A
MESSAGE
OF
Love

A CHANNELLED GUIDE
TO OUR FUTURE

Ruth White with Gildas

To, Joel
with love
and blessings
Sonie & Alan
1995.

PIATKUS

A light is
dawning!

First published in 1994 by
Judy Piatkus (Publishers) Ltd
5 Windmill Street, London W1P 1HF

The moral right of the author has been asserted

A catalogue record for this book is available from the British Library
ISBN 0-7499-1356-8 (pbk)

Edited by Jill Sutcliffe
Designed by Sue Ryall·
Illustrated by Zena Flax

Set in 12/13½ pt Compugraphic Baskerville by
Action Typesetting Limited, Northgate Street, Gloucester
Printed and bound in Great Britain by
Mackays of Chatham PLC

To Mavis Reid, my catalyst, who has
inspired and brought together many people
who otherwise might never have shared
their hopes, dreams, prayers and fears.
With thanks and love.

Contents

Acknowledgements

I have received a great deal of support and encouragement in the writing of this book. I should particularly like to thank the editorial team at Piatkus, for their fostering of creativity.

My daughter Jane is a staunch and loving ally. She has enabled me to take time to write, by taking over many administrative tasks. She also designed the illustrations on pages 54 and 55.

Hugh Dunsford-Wood provided the illustration on page 94. It is one which I use frequently in my work and greatly appreciate.

Tony Van den Bergh, once again, helped me with the script. His humour and love helped me to a sense of proportion.

Members of my workshops and trainings frequently asked the right questions of Gildas, thus stimulating his replies. I thank them for the sensitivity and effort they put into the art of questioning.

Introduction

This is a joint venture between myself and Gildas, my discarnate guide and communicator.

As a young child I was aware of a presence beside me. Although I knew that he was not 'solid', it was some time before I realised that others were unable to see him. He sometimes 'wears' a white robe, like the habit of a Benedictine monk. At other times he appears to me in a 'body' which consists only of energy, light and colour. He is not living an incarnate life on earth, but inhabits another 'plane'. He is, therefore, in a discarnate or disembodied state. His last incarnation was as a French monk in the fourteenth century. Now, from his other plane he teaches and responds to questions which reveal a wider perspective to the personal and general problems which beset us. He has helped many people who are searching for the meaning of life.

I can attune to Gildas' voice and presence very quickly. Words, as in dictation, pour into my mind and I then speak them into a tape recorder or write them down. I am in a dreamlike state and not fully aware of what has been said until I hear or read the words again afterwards.

I was nineteen years old when I first began to receive extensive teachings from Gildas. I had no terminology with which to describe him. I only gradually learned about 'discarnates', 'auras', 'chakras', and 'other planes'. We have now worked together for over thirty-six years and, though I use this sort of language daily, I do not like 'jargon' and have tried to limit it. Some of the subject matter of this book, however, requires a specialist vocabulary. In order to prevent the explanation of terms from interfering with the flow of the text, a Glossary has been added. With this addition I hope that this book can be complete and understandable in itself. For those who want to read more widely, or learn more of Gildas' and my story, other books are suggested in the Bibliography.

Many times in this book there is a need to refer to a Higher Power or Being. The word 'God' can be confusing and unacceptable. It may be seen as sexist, patriarchal, Jewish, Christian or discriminatory. Gildas often substitutes the all-inclusive phrase 'The Source of All Being' or shortens it to 'Source'.

Varying teachings are produced or required for different ages. Throughout history many themes can be traced. As little as fifty years ago, even in the Western world, life was slower and the roles of human beings less complex. Now, in the machine age, each person combines many of the former specialist tasks. Many women, for example, drive cars, use a typewriter, and have a career, in addition to looking after children, and doing housework. It is as though we live more than one life in a normal life-span. The world has somehow 'speeded up'. Change and revolutionary developments of all kinds happen overnight. We are concerned with change; fascinated by it or even frightened by it. People of other ages may have needed less guidance, certainly from discarnate sources. The elders had sufficient time to become wise. People had time to listen, think and meditate. Natural rhythms of time, tide and season governed life more directly. It was easier to be in touch with the Divine. Wise prophets and teachers revealed some of the complex esoteric secrets of the universe. These were relayed to the people through myths, songs and stories, through esoteric systems such as the Kabbalah, Alchemy or Yoga and through Astrology or the cards of the Tarot.

Now, in the midst of speed and change, we need teachings to help us to reconnect with some of the ancient wisdoms, as well as to explain to us the meaning, purpose and potential of change. We need to be shown how to maintain hope amidst so many, seemingly well grounded, fears that we may be on course for disaster and extinction.

When the guides speak of 'ages' they are usually referring to periods of approximately two thousand years, each governed by an astrological sign. Each calendar year divides into twelve astrological phases, and astrologers (not just in the popular magazine style), can give individuals much insight and advice based on the exact time of their birth. The signs are Aries (the astrological year begins around 21 March), Taurus, Gemini, Cancer, Leo, Virgo, Libra, Scorpio, Sagittarius, Capricorn, Aquarius and Pisces.

The signs and planets governing the two thousand year ages move in reverse order and the 'cusp' or change-over point is more difficult to calculate than for our monthly 'zodiac' or 'birth' signs. As we come to the year two thousand we are moving out of the age which was influenced by Pisces, into the age of Aquarius. Our guides tell us that this has the potential to be a 'Golden Age' bringing tremendous mental and spiritual expansion. Our bodies and the substance of matter will change. Disease and ageing will be things of the past and we will learn to live in peace and love with all our fellow human beings.

Alongside changing 'ages', Gildas speaks of 'increasing vibrational rates'. Complex scientific measurement confirms that each different material substance and each of the basic elements essential to life has a distinct and unique 'vibration'. Coarser, denser substances vibrate more slowly than those which are more refined. For instance lead vibrates more slowly than gold.

We are perhaps more familiar with the concept of sound vibrations. Different oscillations or frequencies produce different tones or notes. The vibration, reflection and refraction of light produces varying colours. As the pace of life quickens vibrational changes happen and new discoveries are made as our perceptions sharpen. There is a connection between vibration and perception. We are used to seeing and handling substances and textures within the particular range of vibrations which governs all things material. In colour, our eyes perceive heightened vibrations, as do our ears, with sound and our noses with fragrance. The ability to recognise and be part of an increase in vibrational rates means that an increased range of perception and therefore of experience opens up. The message of love is brought by our guides to help us positively to prepare for such changes. The higher notes in a musical scale build out of and reverberate with, the lower ones. Change and progression must be congruent. When we learn how to aid this congruence we shall be less afraid of our times and more alive to, and excited by, the possibilities they hold.

This book examines some of the issues, hopes and fears arising from such beliefs or teachings and is based on questions which have often been asked of Gildas over recent years and months. I give some explanations and amplifications and Gildas responds, giving his vision and perspective. We also propose some visual and meditative exercises. These are designed to enable us all to take a more active part in bringing about positive change, facilitating personal insights, calming fears and encouraging contact with our guides. They are all produced from Gildas' inspiration combined with my own learning, experience and creativity.

1

The End of the World?

or a New

and Golden Age?

*Why are mediums and 'channellers' in such great demand now? . . .
Who are the 'discarnate communicators'? . . . What is Gildas'
attitude to present world events?*

Common themes in the spiritual belief systems of many
cultures relate to human destiny, major change, catastrophe, the journey to perfection and reunion with the
Divine. The myths, fairy tales, superstitions, ceremonials,
and religious 'climate' or teaching reflect the creeds of
peoples, times and social divisions.

Prophecy and Omens

Prophecy and omens are not explicitly approved in the
Western culture of the 1990s. Yet thousands of astrologers,
palmists, Tarot readers, interpreters of dreams, mediums
and 'channellers' are in great and serious demand. Most
are sincere, sophisticated and well-trained practitioners.

They are consulted about the spiritual meaning, purpose and direction of individual lives. Their comments on the collective fate of humankind and the perennial 'imponderables' are trusted lifelines in a chaotic and changing world.

These consultants, with professional standards and often flourishing practices, are a far cry from the 'fortune teller' whose palm could be crossed with silver in return for prophecy about luck, love, future and fortune – yet the intuitive gifts and sensitivities used in the access of information may be similar. Those who 'see' and have experiences which go beyond the boundaries of immediate reality may be regarded as something of a phenomenon but they have always been in demand and perhaps never more so than now.

A flood of practitioners emerges in response to a need. The interpretation and communication of 'other worldly' insights or intuitions must necessarily have a subjective element. Hence a large amount of material, bewildering to genuine seekers and providing endless fuel for sceptics, agnostics and critics is now in circulation.

There is no doubt that where need produces a market, unscrupulous entrepreneurs will jump on the bandwagon. It is both exciting and worrying to know that the personal growth and New Age movements are rapidly expanding 'industries', even, or may be particularly, in the face of the economic recession of the last few years. The question inevitably arises as to whether the naïve and gullible, or the lonely and bereaved seeking consolation, are being persuaded into selling their souls to those who may cause them to rush, like the Gadarene swine, over the precipice to extinction in the sea. It is ironic that the very fear of extinction gives immense power to all who practise, genuinely or not, in prophecy and guidance.

Discarnate Communications

Particularly bewildering, but increasingly prolific are the messages which come through mediumship and 'channelling'. Communications about the plight and fate of earth and humanity are pouring through from 'discarnate guides', 'ascended masters', 'intelligences from outer space', 'the disciples of Jesus', 'The Virgin Mary', 'Mary Magdalene', 'Jesus Himself', and the 'Voice of God'.

Discarnate communicators (see page 8) often reveal themselves in ancient guise. This is for any or all of the following reasons: they want to attract our attention, have something of importance from a particular tradition to communicate, are appearing in the 'form' they wore in their last earth incarnation, know that the individual they are aiming to contact has an interest in, resonance to, or past life memory of, a particular epoch. There are Native American Indians, Egyptian priests and priestesses, Chinese mandarins, Atlanteans, Nubian slaves, Tibetans, temple dancers, monks, Sisters of Mercy and many more. They speak through ordinary men and women going about their normal lives as well as through professional mediums and channellers. Most bring messages of love, guidance, comfort and wisdom. Some are more threatening, directive or alarmist.

Cults and groups form in order to receive and act on teachings based on a combination of 'the ancient wisdom', and a belief system which includes reincarnation, karma, a complex and hierarchical structure to life 'on the other side' and complete acceptance of the inhabitation of other planets.

Gildas and Ruth

My own journey has been one of a progressive, and now total, involvement with a teaching guide known as Gildas.

I have been aware of his presence since I was a very small child. My parents were conventionally and rather narrowly religious and soon made it clear that perceptions of colour around people (auras), and of nature spirits (fairies), were not only unusual but to be severely discouraged and condemned. Denial of this aspect of my vision led to a crisis with my outer sight. At one period it was thought that I would be blind by my early twenties. Fortunately, at the right time I met Dr Mary Swainson – a student counsellor and Jungian therapist – who was able to validate all my sensitivities and help me to establish strong and clear communication with Gildas.

At first I saw my guide as a monk. The most he has ever told me about himself is that he spent his last life in a monastery in fourteenth-century France. Now, he says he is part of a large group, on the 'other side' who are committed to helping human beings in incarnation. They want to give us a wider perspective of life on planet earth. They teach that change should be welcomed and tell us to prepare to enter 'a New and Golden Age'.

Latterly I perceive Gildas as 'energy' – full of light and colour but without specific form. I have never doubted him to be anything other than a separate being – a distinct universe in his own right and not just an extension of my identity.

I am a natural sceptic and stubborn to boot. Life with a guide has not been easy. Realising and claiming my own identity has been made more complex because of this experience. Yet I cannot deny it or just write it off. I have had to act on it and work with it. Gradually my trust in Gildas as a communicator, respect and love for him as a working companion, and commitment to the work, has grown. A partnership has evolved in which my studies, training and interest in transpersonal psychology go alongside Gildas' teaching about other worlds and states.

As a communicator Gildas is gentle and wise. His view of

our present world events, the plight of humanity and of the earth is positive and full of love. He is critical of complacency and does not hesitate to 'grasp the nettle' when necessary, but he is not alarmist.

Acceptance of Gildas' presence in my life and of myself as a channel for his 'voice' has been made easier because he is not dictatorial. I have never felt that he has wanted to make all my life decisions for me. Neither does he interfere in my personal life, views and opinions. Through the long association and growth of trust I accept most of his cosmology as a working hypothesis but there are times when, after discussion, we agree to differ.

There was an upsurge of interest in channelled teachings around 1967. Many sources spoke of that year as being the one of definitive change. Incarnate seers and discarnate communicators warned of cataclysm, disaster and Armageddon. When I read Gildas' teaching from this time I find it more confrontational than ever before or since. An excerpt from *Gildas Communicates* (1971) reads: 'There will be many – in fact a large majority – who will experience a great sense of shock. All that they now recognize as being "life" and "worth living for" will be wiped out at one stroke. They will be afraid and insecure like small children faced with the loss of all comfort they have ever known.' Yet in comparison to some other communicators he was mild. He took the view that we needed time; that if the changes could come more gradually and be mainly those of human heart and consciousness, then total cataclysm and disaster of a physical nature would be avoided.

The End of a Millennium

Now we are approaching the end of a millennium. It is hardly surprising that dramatic events should be expected and forecast. Should we be full of fear or in a state of excited anticipation? Will our sick and injured planet, in order to survive herself, refuse to sustain the human life which has poisoned and polluted her? In such an event what will happen to us? Shall we be cast into the void or will spaceships from other planets appear to lift us off until it is safe to return once more? Will we *all* be 'rescued'? Is there going to be a great separation of the sheep and the goats as prophesied in the biblical Book of Revelation?

It seems timely to consider these questions and many more; to understand what lies behind them and to ask Gildas for a summary and update of his teachings on those hopes and fears which are of immediate concern to us both individually and collectively.

2

Who is Speaking to

Us and Why?

How do our individual belief systems affect the communication we receive? ... Why are we experiencing our present confrontational era? ... What is the 'work' of guides?

Answers to the question: 'Who is speaking to us and why?' cannot be objectively proven within the present paradigms for scientific research. The receivers of messages and the groups which form around them have a subjective invest- ment in the naming of the communicator. This usually accords with a belief system attractive to the group or indi- vidual. Thus, those to whom Christianity is important but who question some of its confines may be drawn to commu- nicators naming themselves as One of The Disciples, The Virgin Mary, Mary Magdalene, Jesus or The Direct Voice of God. Equally, these very names may seem irreverent and presumptuous to the Christian purist.

Religion, Spirituality and Channelling

Many churches are empty. This does not necessarily mean that spirituality is being shunned. The influx and popularity of 'channelled messages' show that people are still seeking, as ever, for a deeper meaning to life. It is dogma, rather than spirituality which is being questioned; a practice rather than a religion which is being sought. A wider cosmology which includes patterns from traditional Eastern beliefs is attractive to many. Such seekers will be found among the listeners to Native American Indians, Nubian Slaves, Tibetan Dancers, Sisters of Mercy and communicators with names like Gildas, White Flame or Mantis. Such names and personalities suggest a belief in reincarnation, which in its turn presupposes that there is a continued existence or experience on some other plane or in a between-life place. The name 'Gildas' was quite common in mediaeval France. Several place names in Brittany begin or end with 'St Gildas'. It means 'A messenger of truth'.

Acceptance of communication from human voices located on a different plane requires and strengthens belief in survival. The longing to know that life goes on beyond the release of 'this mortal coil' lies deep within us and encompasses not only our greatest hopes but our greatest fears. Belief in messages from other planetary inhabitants or intelligences opens a variety of possibilities. It also gives both hope and fear another dimension.

Most of the names or labels for guidance have an archetypical quality to them, for example, Native American Indians may be called 'Sitting Bull', monks are often known as 'Brother ... (Lucas, Joseph, etc)' whereas Guides appearing in Atlantean form often have names like 'Blue Flame'. The need for this is representational of what we are seeking and why. Things are so out of balance in our world and with the earth that, intrinsically, we know ourselves to be lost. For example, we have an uneven distribution of resources and wealth. There are holes in the ozone layer and global warming. Our seas, rivers and even the air we breathe, are heavy with pollution. We are poisoning ourselves as well as the earth itself. Crime, particularly rape, murder and violence is on the increase. Nation is not at peace with nation. Colour prejudice is rampant. Consequently we seek the original pattern, the blueprint, the archetype, in the hope that we shall recognise, or be set upon our true course once more.

The truly archetypical is difficult for the finite mind to grasp. It carries wisdom and gathers to it collective strength. It maintains a purity and depth and reflects that Divine Source or Knowledge which is mainly accessible through inspiration, meditation, prayer, and 'altered states of consciousness'.

The personification of archetypes in images, symbols, dreams, reflections, stories, myths, astrology and the Tarot is reflective of the struggle of the finite mind to understand them. For example, the major arcana in Tarot consists of twenty-two archetypes, including Death, The World, The Fool, The Hierophant, The Devil, The Lovers or Twins, The Hanged Man, and The Lightning Struck Tower. In an age where we are largely out of touch with mystery and tradition, it is unsurprising and natural that we should give at least some archetypical qualities to discarnate guides and communicators. If they are not strong enough to carry these, then they are unlikely to be true guides.

In time of crisis it is our wont to look to politics or religion to furnish us with strong and inspiring leadership. Figures such as Mahatma Gandhi, John Wesley and Winston Churchill brought inspiration and confidence. Such leaders 'hold' or 'carry' the archetype of leadership without being seduced or corrupted by it. At present no similar leader is forthcoming. We must beware that we do not snatch at straws in our anxiety or, throwing discrimination to the winds, hear only what we want to hear and *cause only that to be communicated*. Our collective expectation has a subtle influence on leaders of the times. When we are confused, our leadership will be confused and collusive.

If we put authority too much outside or beyond ourselves we are diminished and can only be led, taught or rescued. A certain comfort in being naïve and handing over responsibility is at least a part of the reason why we are experiencing our present confrontational era. 'Iron Lady' leaders such as Margaret Thatcher tend to make all our decisions for us. We get the leaders we deserve.

The Continued Existence of Being

I have a belief, first learned from Gildas, in a continued existence of being or essence, though not necessarily of personality. I experience Gildas clearly as another being or intelligence, outside myself, not a part of my psyche or inner life. I accept his basic explanation of who he is (see page 8). I know that he is enabled to speak most clearly through me when I can let go of all my prejudices and fears and listen from an inner place of clarity and receptivity. I also believe that being receptive is not being passive. Within receptivity lives a dialogue where creative discrimination is welcomed.

Having hinted that discarnate communicators may be part of the collective and archetypal bank of wisdom and stated that I doubt the long-term survival of personality, I must hasten to add that most guides reveal great individuality and style in their communications. We come to love and respect them and their vibration. I am convinced that these individual traits are beyond any 'colouring' which it is possible for the channel to put on to the guide. But are they less or more than archetypes? How should we see them? How protect ourselves in our vulnerability without shutting out a wider view or perspective? The prospects of help with our belief or of hands held out to aid us as we stumble, are perennially attractive.

Eventually all we can do is attempt to know ourselves, our prejudices, anxieties and hang-ups and then listen without naïvety, to the guides themselves. If what they have to say and the way in which they present themselves 'suits our condition' and strengthens us, then we may expand our belief system and accept at least a working hypothesis. Greater personal certainty in either direction can only grow through trial and error. In this century, through psychology and psychoanalysis, we have learned to study ourselves. In any interaction with guidance the function of self-observation should never be in abeyance but when a rapidly increasing number of people have similar, albeit subjective experiences something must be happening which requires intelligent attention.

The guidance phenomenon mostly seems to concern the Western world. This is probably because Eastern religions tend to be much more in touch with archetype and myth while the concept of the prophet, holy man or woman, as a bridge to communication with the gods, has remained vibrant and alive.

The following comments and extracts are from Gildas and give his view about who is speaking to us and why. (See the Glossary for specialised terms.)

GILDAS

Origins and evolution

The original spark or soul comes from the Source. In order to become like the Source and also to ensure that the Source is not static, the soul takes on incarnation and journeys through many lifetimes in search of evolution. Gradually an overseeing, observing or higher self emerges and then each time incarnation takes place only a part of the whole becomes personified in order to undergo the further experience which the essence requires in its search for wholeness.

The essence or soul thread is vital, increasingly conscious and eternal. The learning process continues

on other planes of being, between as well as during
lifetimes.

When the soul thread is sufficiently evolved, the
wheel of rebirth is no longer its main concern or focus.
There is then an opportunity to continue on the path of
evolution by being of service in different ways. Guides
and communicators have agreed to help the collective
journey by sharing the less finite view and wider
perspective seen from other planes of being. This is
why we seek individuals on earth with whom to
communicate. Our aim is to help in making the
experience of incarnation less blinkered or limited in
vision.

Guides cross the interface between planes in order to
communicate.

The 'work' of guides

Guides belong to groups, and accordingly have
different concerns or aims in making their contact
with incarnate human beings. For some, the main
focus will be healing, for others teaching, while
others will seek to inspire the artist, poet, architect,
musician or writer.

There is a gentle hierarchy which comes from
assimilated experience. Eventually there can be total
absorption into the Source – but even the Great
Masters or Ascended Ones seek more direct and
constant contact with the earth plane during the
times you are now experiencing. You, and therefore
we, are at a dangerous but exciting point in the
evolution of consciousness.

There are life forms and intelligences on other
planets. Most, but not all, are benign. If there is to be
a big change in any part of the universe, then that
change will affect the whole. The space-beings seek to

give support, but are also interested in preventing the sort of negative reverberation which would happen if planet earth should be destroyed or no longer able to support the human life-force.

Faith in the future

True guidance communications are supportive in the information which is offered. We are all journeying together. Our beings on these planes are more diffuse than are yours on earth. We take on a personality in order to make a more understandable, direct and tender contact with you – but we no longer endure the limitations of personality as you do.

A great and golden opportunity lies ahead. We communicate in order that in spite of the chaotic or even violent experiences you have, you should not lose hope or faith about the future. We bring positive hope for the potential of humankind to live together in light, love and optimum health.

In order that there may be 'breakthrough' many structures have to be released or to break down – both individually and collectively. Holding on to the outworn prevents positive change – though some values are eternally enduring.

The jewel of truth is many faceted. We come to help you in reconciling the opposites and polarities and in understanding the paradoxical.

We seek to communicate from heart to heart on a vibration of love.

3

Why Are We Here?

Where Are We Going?

Is the world going to end? . . . Are we going to destroy the world and ourselves with it? . . . Is there anything we can do? . . . Does individual action really make a difference?

These questions are as old as conscious individuality itself. They are the substance of philosophical and religious debate of all times.

According to some of the guides, we are here simply because we are a part of the whole. Our presence prevents stasis. Through our existence, 'becoming' continues. We are as necessary to the Source of Life as It is to us and in a fundamentally symbiotic relationship with It. Rather than stay innocent and protected we were meant to explore all aspects of life. We are travelling towards a creative state of wholeness in which movement will continue but where the darker side of knowledge will have been voluntarily renounced. The New and Golden Age can only be created and known on earth in fully conscious understanding, in co-creativity with the Source and as a result of experience and exposure. Being protected from knowledge and only allowed to know harmony and light would be a static and eventually futile condition.

Fear that the world will end is primitive and basic. With each sunset the ancients relived their doubt of its return, their fear of darkness, chaos and death. They invented rituals to help the sun to rise again and assure it of its welcome. In this way through active involvement they eventually came to understand and trust the natural rhythms.

Our Present Dilemma

Now we have advanced systems for studying ourselves, the earth and our relationship to it. We have speedy and sophisticated communication systems. We are more aware of the whole of humanity than ever before. We hear about and even see pictures of what is occurring thousands of miles away while it is actually taking place. Few remote unexplored areas or unknown peoples remain. Yet we are increasingly out of touch with the times, seasons and rhythms of our earth. We are even able to alter the natural growth cycles of plants, trees and animals. We see death as failure, fallow periods as waste and put ourselves and nature into stress and overdrive.

Reports about the polluted state of the earth, global warming and holes in the ozone layer are terrifying. The problems are too vast for the average individual fully to comprehend or attempt to overcome. We dutifully separate our paper from other rubbish, re-use supermarket plastic bags, sort brown, green and clear bottles from each other, post them into the marked bottle-bank holes and hope that we are 'doing our bit'.

Our Underlying Fears

But what about the underlying fears? What do we envisage when we think of the ending of the world? Do we imagine a devastating nuclear explosion? A natural catastrophe such as earthquake or flood? Scenes of mass deaths from illnesses like AIDS? Or slow starvation, drying up and suffocating as a result of living in our own toxic pollution of the planet? When we speak of 'the world' do we mean the earth or the universe – or do we not even really think beyond the familiar well-trodden part of the world/earth/universe in which we currently happen to live? Perhaps we hardly dare to think at all?

Gildas urges us to think; not fatalistically, not complacently, but co-creatively.. One of the traps we may fall into is a belief that an anthropomorphic God is punishing us for our wickedness and our failure to look after the earth which was given to us as a precious gift. Putting ourselves in the place of the victim or the naughty child means that there is an underlying expectation that when the punishment is sufficient God will step in and make it all right again. Punishment may be horrid but it has an ending. If we endure it, order will be restored by an outside authority.

'Not so,' say the guides. It is time to stir ourselves; time to see responsibility as something other than a boring word; time to take heart and be creative. Dreaming the hopeful dream and seeing the positive vision should continue, even in the face of the difficulties we encounter, but we must also seriously endeavour to find ways of empowering ourselves to aid their realisation. Individual action and positive attitudes *do* make a difference. It is necessary to remember and relate to the power of what has been called 'the creative minority'. When an optimum but minor number of people change their belief systems and their actions the whole of humanity changes with them. (The optimum number is thought to be around 10 per cent.) The tiny amount of yeast in the batch of dough changes the constitution of the whole.

GILDAS

The complexity of the universe

When you think 'world', try to think 'universe'. In this way bring a sense of proportion to your predicament. Think of your galaxy, think of galaxies beyond that, think of infinity. Know that you are a drop in the ocean.

Think of the complex geometry of the universe. Think of the perfect, intricate balances and harmonies which hold the planets in their courses and determine their relationship to each other. Think of the repercussions and reverberations which would result if earth and/or humanity were to be destroyed. Know that a drop in the ocean is a universe in itself and is in vital relationship to the whole.

These intricate balances and harmonies of the universe are the Divine Manifestation itself. Perfection or the sublime is often assumed by the finite mind to be an end product – finished and whole. It is more difficult to imagine a perfection which is moving and evolving in such a way that even at moments of seeming chaos, the positive creative tension is not lost. The finite mind is bound in time, by the physical behaviours of matter and by linear thought forms and perceptions. In order to find the opportunities which lie within and beyond your present earth experience it is necessary to use the creative possibilities of the imagination. You need to overcome or break through sequential and consequential belief patterns and embrace positive expectation. Three-dimensional reality is solid but limiting – seek to imagine the fourth and fifth dimensions which go far beyond form as you now know it. Such a quantum leap in vision opens new possibilities, begins to activate some of

the unused areas of the human brain and brings
spiritual uplift.

Letting go and moving on

The consequence of the destruction or dropping away
of old patterns is not necessarily death. Healing is not
a return to a state of health previously known but a
breakthrough to a new perception. Disease of all kinds
can be a valuable learning process which ensures
growth and spiritual strength. Reform is not a penal
institution but a golden opportunity to take part in
positive *re-formation*. Punishment is not necessarily
sequential on failure to maintain the old order.

Perfection is not static but dynamic and the human
order is essential to that dynamism. The world is not
going to end but it is going to change. The old order,
the old limitations are going to be overcome.
Vibrational rates are going to change – indeed are in
the process of changing. The constitution of matter
including the human substance is changing.
Everything is speeding up in terms of time dimensional
experience. Consequential thought tends to see the
outcome of too much speed as the irresistible force
meeting the immovable object with the subsequent
destruction of each by the other. Yet is this not also a
form of breakthrough? The clash is not an ending but
a gateway to new experience.

Precipitation into another dimension does not have
to be violent. It is the linear, physically orientated
consciousness which expects it to be so. Where
consciousness does not make the required leap in
imagination then some degree of physical breakdown
may be necessary to force the new horizons into view.
The old structures can hide the new and prevent the
subtle veil from thinning.

We (the guides), do not now expect that there will

be a totally earth-rending cataclysm. We await with
excitement the breakthrough in human consciousness
which will see the subtle solutions, new dimensions
and new orders which are being held out towards
you from other planes of consciousness. These are
coming rapidly into your perspective and love is
the force which is guiding them towards you. Yet
guides, helpers, beings and intelligences from other
dimensions and planets can only make a part of the
journey. You also have to be willing to travel. The
vehicle for this kind of travel is thought governed by
imagination. Do not be drawn into imagining the
worst and preparing for it. While taking full note of
your predicament imagine the best and prepare to
embrace it. Flights of fancy have their own reality and
enable you to cross the interface between the planes of
experience and to know the areas where love has
overcome fear.

Eternal life

You are, of course very aware of your physical bodies
and their limitations. When the body dies it disinte-
grates and rots. The life force has departed from it. But
that life force is eternal – there are other forms of
embodiment. The spirit never dies or fails, its flame
burns on. Every individual essence survives and can
never be destroyed. If consciousness is eternal then the
world – whatever your definition of it may be – is
eternal also. It cannot end, only change. Pain will soon
be something of the past, because the process of
learning and evolution is one of changing patterns,
and the spur of comprehension has been pain. When
matter and the substance of your bodies reach a higher
level of vibration you will move beyond physical pain.
The refined vehicle is not vulnerable to suffering.

Increased vision will reveal more of the universe's beauty and meaning. You will be beyond pain and disease because you will be in constant attunement to the universal laws of harmony and grace.

Individual action

At all levels, from all viewpoints, individual action really makes a difference. Watch, pray and meditate. By all means participate in practical energy conservation exercises but when doing so try not to envisage that you are part of a helpless minority hopelessly endeavouring to stem an overpowering tide. Try not to see these actions either, as aiding a return to patterns previously known. It is necessary to move on, not back. The unknown makes all in the human condition feel insecure. You need therefore to practise visualising a positive unknown, where all burdensome limitations, pain and disease no longer exist.

Seek symbolic meaning. See your personal experience as an integral part of the whole movement towards a goal. Even if you are isolated, confined or in some way imprisoned, light a candle each day and visualise its light as part of a network, joining and illuminating the hearts of all humans everywhere. Such actions work powerfully in the subtle stratospheres and enable positive change.

Meditation to Aid Awareness of
The Network of Light

Try to begin by preparing a quiet space for yourself and lighting an actual candle. Dedicate this light to the network of light, the angels of light or to positive change in human consciousness.

Either sit cross-legged or lotus position or have a chair which allows both feet to be flat on the ground. (Having your feet on a cushion is also acceptable.) Take some time to be balanced and comfortable. Pay particular attention to the alignment of your head and neck as this helps to relieve tensions and to balance the chakras (energy points) within your energy field.

Watch the flame of your candle and be aware of the rhythm of your breathing without trying to change it. After a few moments, close your eyes and focus your breathing into your heart chakra which is on the same level as your physical heart but in the centre of your body.

Imagine a gentle light burning in your heart centre and illuminating all the upper area of your body . . . Imagine that each cell of your body is filled with light and begins to glow, so that you emanate light into the room around you . . . Imagine this gentle light filling your whole house, or the building where you live . . . It reaches out into the street, touches the heart centres of passers-by, who also begin to glow with light and take it with them and pass it on to all whom they will meet . . . The light from your house causes other buildings to be full of light . . . Even the streets and roads, the earth around begins to glow with light . . . Your whole town or village glows with light . . . The light travels on from heart to heart, from place to place until your whole country . . . the whole world . . . the whole of humanity . . . glow with light . . .

When you feel ready to do so, gradually bring your awareness back from the wider imagining to your own street . . . your own house . . . your own room . . . your own body . . . your own heart chakra . . . Become aware of the contact of your body or feet with the ground . . . Open your eyes and be aware of the candle which you lit . . . Visualize a cross of light in a circle of light over your heart chakra, keep a cloak of light around you, and when you blow out the physical candle send the light out in healing to a person or cause which you hold dear.

4

Cataclysms and

Breakdown of Systems

Will there be a shift in the Earth's axis?. . . . What changes should we expect? . . . Do we need to build nuclear shelters? . . . What will happen to the institutions of Church and Monarchy?

Guides often speak to us about letting go of old structures or old orders, of an impending shift in the earth's axis and of the need to take a quantum leap in awareness. Although guides have usually lived many lifetimes on earth, moving on seems to make them forget some of the frailties of the human condition. Mostly they do not intend to be alarmist, but can be out of touch with the apprehension and panic which such statements can engender in the incarnate human breast.

In the last chapter Gildas states that from their viewpoint there is no longer an expectation that some complete catastrophe will destroy the earth in one fell swoop. He often says that disasters will be contained and not worse than any we have already known. In other words he does not see an increase in earthquakes, volcanic eruptions, floods, whirlwinds, hurricanes, droughts, pestilences and scourges. Neither does he predict an immediate *decrease* in so-called natural disasters. The body of the earth itself is changing and we must expect it to shake itself around in order to accomplish this!

Where Some of Our Fears Originate

There is geological and historical evidence of a lost continent known as Atlantis. Its inhabitants misused power and knowledge to such an extent that they were instrumental in bringing about its destruction. This great land mass suffered flooding and inundation. It disappeared dramatically into the sea carrying the population with it.

Jung, the great psychologist, tells us that anything which has ever been known or experienced by human beings is stored in the 'collective unconscious' where it has a certain negative autonomy. There are many creation myths from different cultures and religions which include references to a great flood. Even if we accept that disasters of the kind with which we are already acquainted are an inevitable part of the pattern of change, we need to know whether this might include anything of such magnitude as the sinking of Atlantis. We need to recognise that our fears of losing all that is tangible, all that we hold dear, are not merely free-floating panic symptoms. They are linked to these specific experiences which are imprinted on the collective memory bank. If necessary we need to remind our guides of this and ask them to be explicit about the vision which they see for us.

Death is a part of life. To the time-conscious mind each passing minute is part of the dying process. Every change through which we pass involves a death of the old and a birth of the new. Perhaps because we are in a continuous encounter with symbolic and actual deaths our need for security is extreme. Philosophically we may understand that security is arguably non-existent but the instinct for life preservation is very strong. We yearn for security.

For this reason we find predictions of change disturbing, unsettling or terrifying. We are physically dependent. We need either reassurance or sufficient information to give us the opportunity to make contingency plans.

Faults in the Earth's Crust?

How would gravity be affected by a shift in the earth's axis? Are we likely to fall off the planet? We are aware of various 'faults' in the earth's crust such as the Andreas fault in California – if the shift is violent will these be aggravated or give way and cause the flooding we dread?

Already, groups of people have made contingency plans of various kinds. Some of these are in the hands of official bodies – others are the initiative of New Age groups acting on their beliefs or on interpretation of what they have heard from guides. In London we have the Thames barrier, a defence resulting from surveyors' fears of horrific flooding in which the sewerage systems would break down, leaving not only the havoc which water can wreak but all the problems of rampant infection connected with uncontained effluent.

Official nuclear shelters have been built. Private groups of worried families have contributed to build their own versions of these, fully stocked with survival supplies.

In California people have moved from low-lying houses and have started communities and townships in the mountains, out of reach of possible flood waters.

Should we all be taking the threat to our future existence so seriously? Should there be a concerted human effort to change the nature, structure and location of our settlements?

What of governments? Institutions of Church and monarchy worldwide? They are all part of known systems and order – will they too break down? Are they even now in the process of bringing about their own redundancy? In Britain, for example, we are familiar with the 'skeletons' which emerge almost daily from the royal and governmental cupboards. The Church too is failing in its duty to provide guidance and leadership over these and many other issues.

Known order, even when we are dissatisfied with it, induces security. Things which are unpleasant and painful can make us feel safe so that we seek them out again and again for reassurance. Something very attractive may lie ahead, within our grasp, but how often do we turn back to the known instead of eagerly seizing the opportunity? All change encompasses a dread of the void or an element of chaos. We fear chaos as we fear evil. The two words are often synonymous for us. Yet evil may be extremely ordered as in Nazi Germany. It usually depends on domination, which leads to harsh rules and petty observances. Recent research shows us actually on film how chaos seeks a new order which is in fact already held within its intricate patternings and great beauty.

The Chinese word for crisis is made up of two glyphs. The first on its own, means 'danger' – the second, 'opportunity'. It seems that we must be aware of the dangers of our present predicament but overcome them by looking firmly towards the opportunities.

Here are Gildas' responses to these issues:

GILDAS

It is helpful when we are able to have a dialogue with you. In the dimensions which we inhabit we are beyond the limitations of time and the body. We try to identify as closely as possible with your feelings and your predicament but in some respects we need your guidance almost as much as you need ours. If there is a true dialogue, in which you listen to our statements and then tell us your response and your needs, then the bridge between the planes of experience can become stronger and stronger.

From the perspective which we see from this side we put great importance on the interdependence or symbiosis between the intrinsic life force of earth and that of humanity. This is so strong that anything which takes place in the body of earth affects the body of humanity, not only through the obvious, necessary reactions and accommodations which must be made to physical changes but in the sense that mutation in the substance of one, causes or enables the same in the substance of the other.

Flowing with change

The ancient martial arts, such as Tai-Chi, Aikido and Karate, show that when there is flow with the energy which is already in motion, greater momentum is achieved. Resistance is energetically uneconomical. Earth in its instinctual consciousness will flow with the natural energies of evolution but will also, from the same instinctual consciousness assert its survival mechanisms. If humanity flows with the need to change, evolution will be harmonious and sympathetic. If humanity resists or refuses the momentum of change, then the logical consequence could be that earth will break the symbiotic bond in order to follow its own natural sequence and survival. Its environment could become incompatible with the physical needs of incarnate humanity. Earth has instinct. Humanity has free will. Where that free will blocks change, earth will tend to force the issue through elemental eruptions. Where the free will embraces change and moves beyond its present tunnel vision, then cataclysms will cease and 'the desert will blossom like the rose'.

Geological study tells us that there have already been numerous changes in the angle of the earth's axis. These have played an active part in the evolution of humankind, gradually enabling and requiring a new perspective and a more responsibly conscious relationship to the universe. Obviously a sudden and significant shift in the earth's axis could activate such changes in the crust as to be threatening to human incarnate survival in its present form.

If human consciousness were to flow with such a shift in earth's axis then universal awareness of new dimensions would be precipitated. Likewise, if there is a shift in the axis of human thought and spirituality, no sudden and over-dramatic alteration in the earth's axis will be necessary.

Instinct must no longer be separated from creativity or thought from spirituality. When realigned, new dimensions can be more universally perceived. Such separation means that human solutions to the present difficulties follow the physical dimension too closely. The subtle worlds and energy fields are not taken seriously enough; scientific frames of reference are not extending quickly enough. The creative minority, who believe in and explore the subtle worlds, are too facilely labelled 'eccentric but harmless'.

Letting go of fear

The truth is that the planet is in a process of irreversible change. It is not possible to return to the past. It is not destruction and the void which lies ahead but a whole new range of potential and experience. The Divine Plan is full of love and beauty. Beyond the guilt, the fear, the violence, which you tend to hold now in uppermost consciousness, there is harmony, peace and new positive potential.

We are aware that the fear of inundation and destruction is imprinted in the collective unconscious of humanity. The myths of such events are not only symbolic but reflect experience. Most also contain a symbol of promise. In the Biblical version of the story of the great flood the symbol of the rainbow is of great importance. It is a convenant or promise, a bridge between different realms. In the colour spectrum different vibrational possibilities are revealed. Each colour frequency belongs to a different plane of experience and there are other scales of colour notes beyond the ones you now see and know. There is promise within the universe, not threat. Your thinking patterns and your realities will shift and you must be receptive to the possibilities.

Once the thought patterns change, nothing physical can or will harm you any more. You will no longer be dependent on the present physical laws for survival and sustenance.

The process of change

It is easy for we who are beyond the physical plane to say these things. Inevitably you will ask: 'But what about the actual process of change? Even if we overcome the fear of change we are still anxious about the transitional phase.' This is understandable. The desire to build nuclear shelters and set up communities in high mountains is natural. There is even a certain wisdom in the urge to preparedness which results in these actions. Yet such physical readiness emerges from your present thought forms and experience.

The process of change will not be more difficult, painful or undignified than anything you have previously experienced. This is part of the promise held within the symbol of the rainbow. You are having many more difficulties now than could possibly be experienced in breaking through to a new dimension. It is not only that nothing will be worse than you already know, much will be better than you know.

You will be free of disease; free of the ageing process; free of limitation; free of disability and pain; free of greed and jealousy and full of the experience of abundance, joy and love (see page 106).

Try not to waste your resources in building nuclear shelters or moving to high mountains. The thought form of expectation is very powerful. Use the urge to be ready to fuel your imagination to expect the states of health and freedom I have mentioned. Survival can often become selfish. When you realise that all will live you can afford to be generous. When you relate to the eternity of being, then preservation of the physical status quo is no longer all-important. You can stop focusing on faults in the earth's crust and trust in continuity, especially if you can visualise that continuity as life which is infinitely more satisfying.

Part of our task is to aid the quantum leap in vision, thought and imagination. Part of it is to build such a bridge to your plane that we can actually be instrumental in helping you to negotiate the process of change with celebration and joy.

Although it is possible to come to the logical conclusion that planet earth might cease its symbiosis with humanity and become inhospitable to the human race, this conclusion is again based on known thought patterns or expectations. Sustaining the present vibrational level of life may become impossible, but the earth will remain as the planet of choice. Incarnation will continue, but the laws of matter will expand. The Golden Age body is a body mutated to a higher vibrational level, and we must work together to make that mutation positive and beautiful. The plan of the universe is inclusive, not exclusive.

Chaos and evil

In your thinking, try to separate chaos from evil. See it rather as the breaking up of a mosaic. The pieces are not lost, but when the mosaic is reassembled a new factor or perspective, not recognised before, enables something to emerge which was previously inconceivable. Thus the new order is truly new, emerging from what has been known before, but beyond it in every way.

Governments, Churches and Monarchies have become bound by old orders. The concept that all office involving government and guidance should be held only by spiritual adepts has been lost. Thought and spirit have become separated. The old order must die in order to allow the new to be born.

Again, try not to be drawn into the fear patterns around being without an establishment. Instead look within. Find the inner leader, priest or priestess and monarch. Every human being carries the capacity for integrity and spiritual alignment. It has been too long assumed that 'they' will take all the responsibility.

Another gap which must be reconciled is that between the leaders and the led. It is time to relate not to power but to empowerment. When this relationship is active, then the group empowers good leaders and the leaders, in turn, empower the group. Corruption is eschewed. Leaders and led work together towards a vision which is constantly renewed and in harmony with an altruistic view of human potential.

In truly spiritual peoples, like some ancient Egyptian dynasties and the ancient Israelites, kings and queens are chosen and anointed by those who have the vision to see true destiny; priests and priestesses are scrupulously trained in the mysteries and acquire the strength to stand at the interface between the Divine

Light vibration and that of earth; rulers and priests/priestesses are initiates. They have been through the personal testing time which enables them, through true ritual, to bring the experience of Divinity into each human heart; to keep its flame alive in each individual. Leaders too, come to their task through dedication, commitment and vision. They do not seek temporal power for its own sake, but carry it responsibly, make personal sacrifices in honour of it and offer it as a gift of love to the people for whom they care. The priests of a true church or temple watch the spiritual boundaries and challenge rulership or leadership when there is any intimation that the shadow side of power may be creeping in. Above all the true church neither competes for political power nor stores up over-abundant wealth while many of its flock are struggling with oppression, poverty and starvation.

In Western society most of these values and the esoteric knowledge behind them have been lost. Corrupt systems, by their very definition must break down. If each individual cultivates personal integrity, then eventually the breakdown of systems will lead to the re-establishment of spiritual leadership. Ideally, ceremony as enabling and empowering ritual, will remain; celebration will be important but pomp and circumstance and hierarchies based on false power will be eradicated.

Meditation to Help in Overcoming
Fears of Breakthrough

Make sure that you won't be disturbed. Sit in a cross-legged or lotus position or in a chair where your feet may rest comfortably on the floor. (Use a cushion for your feet, if the chair is not a comfortable height.)

Be aware of the rhythm of your breathing . . . just observe it without trying to change it in any way . . . Gradually imagine that each in-breath and out-breath is coming from your heart chakra (see Chapter 8, page 93 and Glossary) . . . Each breath is helping to activate your heart energy . . .

Travel on the heart breath into your inner space and find yourself in a meadow . . . Take the opportunity to activate all your inner senses, so that in the meadow you see the colours and the objects . . . you hear the sounds . . . you smell the fragrances . . . touch the textures . . . and taste the tastes . . . There is a warm golden sunlight falling on the meadow which also spotlights a pathway leading upwards into the nearby hillside . . .

You decide to follow this path and for a while you enjoy the abundant landscape through which it passes . . . The colours seem exceptionally bright and lovely, the air particularly fresh, the birdsong particularly sweet . . . Now there is a turn in the path and you enter a more desolate part of the landscape . . . the sun is not so warm . . . the vegetation is sparse . . . Ahead it seems the pathway may be blocked . . . a closed gate or a massive rock is in the way, but the light is so lacking now that it is difficult to see what the blockage is . . . It is cold . . . you feel a tinge of uneasiness . . . You decide to keep going at least as far as the blockage, so that you can see it more clearly, though with each step forward a part of you knows that it would gladly turn around and retreat . . . You know that you can do this if you really want to and, looking back towards the meadow you feel reassured to see it still bathed in warm golden sunlight . . .

As you approach the blockage the scene darkens . . . You can hardly see, but just at the moment when it seems you will have to stop or go back, a soft light appears to guide you . . . Looking towards the source of this light you see an angel or guardian . . . You see that the blockage is in fact a great strong gateway which appears to be solidly shut, almost welded together . . . There seems little hope of going on beyond it, but now you are determined at least to touch it . . . to reach this boundary . . . The angelic light goes on illuminating the way for you and you feel safe because of the angelic guardianship presence . . .

As you come to the centre of the gateway, where it seems so firmly welded together, to your surprise it begins to open . . . the angel or guardian invites you to step through . . . and when you do so, you enter a magical world . . . colours are really brighter, there are shades you have never seen before, wondrous plants grow here, wild animals are gentle and tame, the fragrances are new but healing and revitalising, the sounds in the air are sweetly blended and a wondrous fragrance permeates every part of your body . . . You feel healed and whole, free and vitally alive . . .

You look back through the gateway and the former landscape which seemed so beautiful looks like an old black and white film set . . . you want to go forward, not back . . . Gently the angel or guardian tells you that it is not yet time to go forward or remain here . . . you must go back, but if you pick a flower from here and take it back with you, then you will bring some of the light, healing and harmony from this place in your landscape to the more known and familiar parts . . . Now you know where the gateway is and that it opens when you approach, you can cross the threshold more often and bring back some of its light and beauty to enhance your vision of the known . . .

When you are ready, gradually travel back to the meadow . . . As you travel it ceases to be black and white and is colourful and harmonious once more . . . you touch anything which seems jaded or dying with the flower from beyond the gateway and some of the harmony you glimpsed there permeates the familiar landscape . . . Return to an awareness of your breath in your heart centre . . . To an awareness of your body on your chair or the floor . . . To contact with your familiar everyday surroundings . . to your usual reality and the tasks which await you . . . Visualise putting a cloak of white light, with a hood right around you, so that the light you now carry will touch all you meet and you will not be vulnerable and unprotected yourself.

5

Messages from

Outer Space

*Will space-ships come to our rescue? . . . Will there be judgement –
a separation of the 'sheep' from the 'goats'? . . . What, if any, will
be the role of planet earth in the new order? . . . What can we do?*

In recent years there has been an influx of communications
purporting to come from beings on other planets. Some say
a gigantic rescue operation is being planned by friendly and
concerned extra-terrestrials. Space ships will come at the
right moment, gather us up and take us, like refugees, to a
safe place either in this galaxy or another.

The communicators of such messages identify themselves
as beings from other planets and speak through human
mediums or 'channels'. When questioned about the
mechanics of the rescue operation, some hierarchical
selection for seats in the space-ships is usually implied.
Those who strive to live the spiritual life will be rewarded.
They will be kept safe on another planet and helped to
change still further. When earth has cleared herself of the
toxins caused by the human race and becomes habitable
again, the chosen few will be returned to co-create and
participate in an Utopian Golden Age.

These communications come from a confused belief
system. They also raise questions about the fate of those
who are not rescued or 'lifted off'. They sow seeds of hope

and fear at one and the same time. As human beings we have a propensity for creating 'them and us' syndromes in both social and spiritual orders. Many religious groups operate on a principle of 'the chosen few'. 'Are you saved?' is the blunt question of the proselytiser. All must be given the chance to 'hear the word and repent' yet the band of the faithful has a tendency to complacency as it smugly contemplates the fate of the inconvertibles. Punishment, reward, rigidity, fear and power are the foundation stones of such tenets. The picture of a judgemental God issuing favours to the élite, dies hard.

Reference to the incongruity of a belief in life eternal while over-emphasising the preservation of the body and status quo has already been made (see page 34). To put hope in some massive lift-off operation is a too literal solution, probably influenced by science-fiction. It is not a large enough leap forward in imagination.

'Colouring' in Mediumship and Channelling

In mediumship and channelling there is an ever present danger of 'colouring'. In the more conscious, co-operative communications of the Aquarian Age (see page 3), the mental set of the channel or receiver may greatly influence what is being said. Guides and space beings alike can only find their words within the vocabulary range of the channel. The complexities of communication from one plane to another are immense. Thoughts and concepts beyond our normal patterns or expectations are often being transmitted. We have only to remember the game of 'whispers' at a party or dinner table to imagine the range of distortion possible.

Realise also that we all have unconscious or psychological resistances which affect what we are able to hear and it becomes clear that all mediumship or channelling must be wisely interpreted and often symbolically understood.

Thus the idea of lift-off and rescue by 'aliens' has other levels of meaning. As might be expected, some of these particular communications have developed and expanded. The true discarnate or extra-terrestrial messenger/teacher is very skilled. Beginning with the more familiar, we are, in the true educational sense, led forward into expansion of ideas and awareness. Some listeners may prefer to stay with the idea of space-ships and the amazingly complex arrangements these would entail, but where audiences have been willing to extend their belief system the teachings have changed and matured.

The extra-terrestrials, like Gildas and some other well-known teaching guides, tell us that 'lift off' (*not* escape) is not a purely physical happening, but a major breakthrough in awareness. Other dimensions surround us constantly and with a change in mind-set we can inhabit them immediately. The fourth dimension infers a different relationship to time which, added to the three spatial dimensions, greatly increases the permutations of vision, experience and under-standing. It has only been spoken of in relatively recent times and many of us know it at most as descriptive of some-thing which is beyond the realm of ordinary experience.

If we then stretch ourselves to imagine a *fifth* dimension, which perhaps includes a new relationship to sound, colour and fragrance as well as to space, time and thought, the increase in possibilities can seem dizzyingly confusing.

We have to 'sit loose' to such concepts, or as Coleridge put it 'suspend our disbelief', but if we do so it is possible to glimpse how immense change could happen literally between one blink of an eyelid and the next.

Expansion of Consciousness

Physiologically it has been established that only an approximate 3/10ths of human brain cell capacity is developed and active. Looking at our own evolution we can get some idea of the known pace of the journey of expansion. A quantum leap in consciousness, happening quickly and activating more of our capacity would have tremendous momentum and move us into a dramatically expanded consciousness. The ponderous light years, which, in our present time constrictions, separate us from other parts of the universe, would be bridged by a thought capacity set free from the confines of known physical law.

Where there is evolution and unrealised potential, change is inevitable and consequent; where life force is eternal there is no need to escape. Many of the guides tell us time and again: 'In whatever state of being you may find yourself, whether you physically die or not, you will always be in the right place at the right time. Work on your fear of death. Stop trying to engineer physical preservation and you will more easily glimpse the potential ahead.'

It is unlikely that all human beings will be ready for change at the same time. Some separation or selection seems inevitable – but it does not have to be that of the 'sheep' and the 'goats'; neither does it have to be made by selection committee or even a Supreme Being. It does not have to depend on gaining the right number of 'Brownie points'. Those who need more time to make the 'quantum leap' do not have to be left to die of toxicosis or be cast off into outer space, their essence never to be redeemed again. We are *all* eternal beings.

Beyond the time dimension opportunity does not run out. Rhythm takes over from categorical death. In a way which we find most difficult to understand, past, present and future exist together. When just 10 per cent of the population is more open to change and less rigidly dependent on structure, the leap forward can be accomplished without violence, cataclysm and mass destruction.

So, again, the questions arise. What should be our

attitude to extra-terrestrials? How best can we help
ourselves and each other to be ready to seize opportunity?
When other dimensions are easily accessible to us will the
relationship between humanity and planet earth have
outlived its usefulness? Can we have more reassurance
about the process of change and its effect on our physical
bodies?

GILDAS

Extra-terrestrials

Expand your vision of 'the world' to include the
universe – take one step further and realise that
within the vastness of that universe it is unlikely that
earth is the only planet supporting intelligent life form
and it is a very small step further to a belief in extra-
terrestrials. These beings have different bodies to
support their existence and are not bound by your laws
of time and space. Many understand more of the
nature of the universe and infinity than it is presently
possible for you to comprehend with the finite mind.
This is not to say that the minds of extra-terrestrials are
non-finite, but they *are* dissimilar. Many have things to
teach those who inhabit earth, but humans have things
to teach them too. Do not fall into the trap of making
yourselves feel inferior or impotent in the face of that
which is merely different.

There are extra-terrestrials, with wider vision, who
are concerned about the present plight of planet earth
and the 'mistakes' which humanity has made. The
balance in the universe is so finely tuned that any great
cataclysm or destruction on planet earth would have a
vast 'knock on' effect throughout the galaxy. Thus,
beings from other planets have self-interest in

preserving earth and in helping humanity to a wider understanding.

For aeons of time (as experienced on earth), extra-terrestrials have been seeking ways of overcoming the barriers and difficulties in making communication with humanity. Now, as is right and appropriate in a time of need, they are beginning to break through. Sightings of what you call 'unidentified flying objects' have been made over many years and are becoming more frequent. These sightings represent the first stages in a breakthrough in perception. As your belief systems expand, so will your ability to perceive. Openness to possibility precedes discovery. Where something is deemed impossible it will often remain unperceivable.

Friend or foe?

You often call extra-terrestrials 'aliens' – as indeed in some senses they are. In that term there is an implied judgement or evaluation. It is no more right to assume that all beings from other planets are friendly than it is to expect them all to be hostile. Beings with extended perceptions are most usually concerned for the well-being of the whole. They tend to be nearer to a concept of unconditional love and are less fearful and defensive than are humans. They may, however want to impose their solutions and interfere with the free will of humanity, simply because they see the wider picture. A certain amount of forceful drive may be experienced from them where they sense your vulnerability and uncertainty. This is why you must all work at being centred and at expanding the parameters of your vision so that your choices are seen clearly.

No matter how benign and well-intended a

proposed 'lift off' operation may seem, do you really want to be in the position of the rescued or the ingratiated, which can so easily become that of the victim?

There are many complexities. I have stated elsewhere that trust in the perfection and patterning of the universe is essential. Yet there are different kinds of trust and you should avoid being naïve. To some extent naïvety has led you to your present plight. You have made actions without sufficient consideration of the consequences. Trust in yourselves and your place in the total pattern is vital.

You also need to understand that the planet earth is not the centre of the universe, but it *is* the planet of choice and this makes it unique.

Your attitude to extra-terrestrials should be one of openness to friendship and co-operation. You should certainly be willing to accept the existence of such intelligences. Be willing to have a dialogue, be willing to exchange, be willing to listen, be willing to be helped. Yet you should also maintain dignity. Expect to build up a communication as between equals. In so doing you will maintain a hold on your integrity and your discrimination.

If your fear of physical discomfiture disposes you to accept rescue with immediately open arms, at any price and on a competitive basis with others of the human race, then little progress can be made. Now is the time when you all need to think deeply about true human values, human respect, human potential and true brother/sisterhood. Co-operation and the will to deep understanding will help you to succeed. Extra-terrestrials who really have your welfare at heart will understand and want to work with you to make breakthrough joyful and harmonious.

If you flow with the rhythm there will be little

physical discomfort. If you really come to terms with the meaning of eternal life you will cease to fear extinction and know that you will be in the right place at the right time, in the right state at the right time and on the right plane or planet at the right time. You need to work at spiritual understanding so that you can overcome the panic which the physical instinct of self-preservation can engender. Spirituality can help you to an over-view: from the personal to the trans-personal; from anxiety about self to selfless concern for the collective.

Some of our descriptions of change and of the fifth dimension, where there is freedom from pain, disease and ageing, must indeed sound like a sort of heaven or non-material existence, thus making you question the future usefulness of incarnation and planet earth. The material level will still exist, though it will be refined. The qualities of the fifth dimension, as experienced while in incarnation on planet earth, will be mainly qualities of mind and ability, thought and imagin-ation, possibility and opportunity.

I have said that the planet earth is unique because it is the planet of choice and will remain so. One of your greatest debates in the fields of philosophy and religious dogma has always been about free will and predestination or preordination. It is difficult to realise that pre-knowledge of how events will turn out, and therefore the possibility of arranged synchronicity, is not the same as pre-arrangement of the original events. Knowledge of what a choice will be does not interfere with the free will within that choice. Because choice is real, on some levels only a proportion of the future can be seen.

Evil and the shadow

Wholeness must include a knowledge of evil and the shadow. The myth (and I use the word 'myth' in the sense of a story which encapsulates great truths in symbolic form) of the Garden of Eden is often interpreted in such a way as to see the 'fall' and the eating of the fruit of the Tree of Knowledge as a sin. This interpretation has had a considerable part in demeaning not only women but the feminine principle itself.

Such interpretations are judgemental and separatist. The acceptance of the path of knowledge and choice needs to be seen as a courageous and necessary part in bringing the nature of wholeness into full consciousness. You now live in an age where good and evil are being acted out openly. This means that in seeing the nature of evil, there can be a choice as to whether it should continue to be part of experience. It is too easy to give the dark side power and to become impotent and injured by its onslaught. This is a time for choice indeed. Every individual needs to look within, to root out every dishonest and self-seeking thought and to reject it as being unworthy within human potential.

When enough people do this (the creative minority again) then the whole will change. Evil will have been experienced and rejected. It will no longer be accepted as a means of expression. Its life-force will be withdrawn.

Thought forms are powerful. They give life and produce manifestations. When you fear evil you give it power and vitality; when you refuse to entertain it you withdraw its life-force. This does not mean that you deny its existence or refuse to face the fact that it is there but that knowing it, as you do in your age, you identify it, name it and reject it.

Evil cannot be overcome by locking it behind bars or pushing it underground. Its defeat must start with the individual, with spiritual growth and with real vision of goodness, harmony and perfection. These things must be seen as a human right, not as the prerogative of privileged individuals or select groups but as something which the collective can and will attain.

There is no need for greed, for anxiety about saving one's own skin, for stock-piling and seeking escape. Breakthrough into the truly perfect means there is enough for everyone, a place for everyone, a love for everyone. Beware of messages, from extra-terrestrials or other guides which contain any encouragement to be exclusive and privileged rather than inclusive and equal. Such messages are usually 'coloured' in the channelling. The exclusive group stands apart, the creative minority changes the whole.

After the changes

Beyond the changes, we see planet earth as a place of peace and opportunity; a place where unconditional love and free will go hand in hand and where there can be that shared spiritual knowledge which enables the correct relationship to material abundance. It *will* be a sort of Utopia where continuing knowledge of the responsibility of choice abides and where the benefits of having chosen to 'seal the door where evil dwells' can be reaped in a physical consciousness which is not possible on any other plane or planet.

That this will come about is foreknown. The choices which will enable it to happen are the choices of free will. Yours!

Meditation to Enable Increased Awareness of the Essential Self

Make sure that you won't be disturbed. Sit or lie comfortably with your body balanced and symmetrically arranged. Be aware of the rhythm of your breathing and let it become quiet and unforced.

Become aware of your body . . . Feel its contact with the chair, couch or floor . . . Feel the texture of the clothes you are wearing not only by touching them with your hands but by knowing their contact with the whole of your body . . . be aware of any bodily discomforts you have . . . any feelings of unease with your body shape or bodily functions . . . Acknowledge the autonomous systems of your body . . . blood flow, immune system, cleansing, eliminative and digestive processes . . . your heart beat . . . your breathing . . . Acknowledge all these things and then say to yourself 'I am more than my body' . . .

Become aware of your emotions . . . Now you may be beginning to feel peaceful, but you may have touched into some deep feelings about your body . . . allow them to be . . . watch them . . . Review your day, working backwards from this moment . . . What emotions have you known today? . . . Joy? Anger? Sadness? Contentment? Jealousy? Bitterness? Grief? Irritation? Peace? Pleasure? Hatred? Love? Do not judge these emotions, just acknowledge their presence in your life and your ability to feel them . . . let them pass and say to yourself, 'I am more than my emotions' . . .

Become aware of your thoughts, your philosophies, your wishes and desires . . . Review as many of the thoughts you have been aware of today as possible . . .

acknowledge their presence in your life . . .
acknowledge the power of your mind . . . then relax in
its presence and say to yourself 'I am more than my
thoughts, more than my mind'. . .

Feel light and non-attached . . . feel the essence of
self which goes beyond body, emotions and mind . . .
sense its quality and perhaps its colour . . . welcome it
as the flame of your eternal being . . . let it refresh you
and heal you for a while . . . Put a cloak of light with a
hood around you before you take up your usual tasks
once more.

6

Individual and

Collective Suffering

Can we have a clearer idea of the belief-system or cosmology from which many of the channelled teachings come? . . . How can we be helped to understand the purpose of: war; AIDS; crime; violence; evil and the shadow?

We live many incarnations. Life is eternal. We experience other planes between each lifetime. Why then do we not know more about our previous lives? Why do we understand so little about the science of the universe as a whole?

We learn through experience. Intelligence enables us to use what we have learned in one situation to help us solve the problems of a completely new set of cirumstances. With accumulated learning we may avoid certain confrontations altogether. If we brought all our knowledge, consciously into each life, we might block many of our own pathways to learning by knowing too much. Where intelligence failed us but memory was strong we might become blocked by ingrained thought patterns, fears or prejudices. Such blockages to our own progression accumulate in the course of one lifetime. Perhaps it is a blessing that with each incarnation the slate is comparatively clean.

As we progress, and as the promised changes draw nearer, past life memories are becoming more common. A vast collective experience has been acquired. We now need to draw on wider memory, knowledge and understanding in order to take an active part in designing and enabling change. Our guides are also our mentors, helping us not only to learn anew, but to remember what has gone before and to evaluate that knowledge with compassion and self-respect.

Now this chapter is entirely in the hands of Gildas.

GILDAS

I do not intend to get caught up in exploring theories about the beginning of the world or the birth of humanity and matter. I shall, however, describe cosmology speaking from my own experience. You must accept that this viewpoint cannot be final or categorical. As guides we are not omniscient. Existentially, compared with you, we are at a different point of evolution and experience. We are free from the time dimension. We see things from a wider perspective and it is from this changed trajectory that I offer my vision.

The soul's journey

When a human soul begins its journey it is a spark which splits off from the Source and chooses human incarnation as its destiny. As it begins its journey of evolution which will, eventually, lead it back to the Source, the spark partially splits once more. The yin, or feminine of its essence, splits from the yang or masculine. These two essences will take different but complementary and interdependent journeys. Each part is like a stem joined at the root or like two strands on a necklace joined at the fastening. Each flower which each stem produces will represent an incarnation. The beads on each strand of the necklace represent opportunities for incarnation. Although basically one stem or strand is yin and the other yang this does not mean that flowers from the yin stem or beads from the yin strand will always undergo or choose feminine incarnation, nor will those from the yang essence always take on a masculine body – but, at the deepest level, they will carry either a stronger yin or stronger yang, imprint.

*The beads
on the strand*

Twin souls

The longing for the twin soul is well known. When evolution is complete, which means that all the beads on the thread have incarnated and returned, the two strands or stems will become one again. During incarnation, until that is possible, a flower from one stem or a bead from one strand may meet with a flower or bead from its twin essence, but twin souls do not always incarnate at the same time.

The complete being does not incarnate. The flowers from the stems or the beads from the threads are aspects of the essential soul. As many as seven aspects from each stem or strand may be incarnate at any one time and if they meet will have a very close relationship. Again, this meeting is rare, since the purpose of incarnation is to gain experience. The impulse behind putting out more than one aspect at a particular period is to ensure as broad a knowledge of that historical earth era as possible. The number of beads on a thread or flowers on a stem varies from soul to soul.

The flowers on the stem

Masculine and feminine/Yin and yang

The main divine principle is that of creation. Yin and yang energies interacting together bring about the birth of the new. Part of the purpose of evolution for human beings is to understand, experience and

therefore use in a balanced way these sacred and divine
energies. The taking on of a gender is one of the ways
in which this learning happens. Since each stem or
strand is slanted towards one principle or the other and
since it is possible for twin souls and soul aspects to
meet in incarnation bearing the same gender, homo-
sexuality takes on a different connotation. These
things are part of experience, part of exploration, not
manifestations which need to be judged or categ-
orically ruled as abnormal, unnatural and dangerous.
When a person, on their journey through life
understands that they and others need all kinds of
experience, then a broad-based compassion and
tolerance develops more easily.

The overall purpose of evolution

There have been periods in your history where it was
more common for twin souls to meet, such as in
Atlantean, Egyptian, Grecian or Native American
Indian incarnations. In the present time a lot of work
is often taken on during the course of one incarnation
and this means that meeting with twin souls is
discouraged by the karmic advisers and helpers. The
danger is that the two beings may be so absorbed in
each other that the degree to which they move forward
their learning process is lessened. When the changes
have taken place it will be *usual* for twin souls to be
working together in incarnation once more. Now, the
range of available experience is very great and twin
souls must live separately in order to cover as much
ground as possible.

The overall purpose of evolution is for the soul to
reunite in full consciousness with the Source of all
Being. Humanity has chosen the path of knowledge.
Unless all experience has been explored and

understood, the journey back to the Source cannot be complete. The Golden Age is not a boon granted by an omnipotent power. It is brought about through human knowledge and choice. When all the options are known then those which enable the best and most harmonious quality of life can be selected and all those which are negative can be eschewed.

The shadow is a combination of the unknown, the undifferentiated and the inadmissible. It is this last category which causes powerful, seething autonomous force. Where there is a refusal to acknowledge everything which exists, or to confront that which is negative, a particularly unpleasant kind of chaos, dissociation and disintegration will reign. Informed choice becomes impossible. Clarity goes into redundancy.

Let me return then to the point at which the soul stem or strand puts out a flower or bead as a personality into incarnation. As experience builds, clearer choices can be made. Until the soul stem builds up data and wisdom, a law of innocence will operate. The love impulse which fundamentally governs the universal patterns does not allow the untried and untested to plunge into incarnations which are full of complex difficulties and horrors. Gradually the strand on which the beads are threaded or the stem which nurtures the flowers, will take a more active part in choosing those incarnations most valuable to its continued evolution. The force which is known as karma or 'cause and effect' becomes active.

A personality bead or flower goes into incarnation, lives out its life span and dies. In the between-life state which takes place on the astral plane, personality bead and soul thread consider the scope of experience gained and assess all aspects of the harvest which has been reaped. It is on the basis of this assessment that the next life is chosen. A new personality bead prepares to incarnate. Its first brief will be to continue to broaden the scope of experience but it will also carry the knowledge that certain things which may have been out of balance because of choices made during incarnation by the previous bead, need to be rectified or redeemed. The incarnating being, then, will carry a motivation to avoid some types of experience, to embrace others and to confront others.

Planning our incarnations

The choice of historical time, social standing, type of body, parents and siblings will have been made by the higher self to expedite the purposes and tasks of the incarnating being. This includes awareness of other higher selves sending personality beads or flowers into incarnation at a similar time. There may be agreement about helping each other with lessons to be learned or experience to be gained. Where there is a group soul purpose, this will be taken into account so that members of the same group or family can facilitate the group learning process by incarnating together. The higher selves making these plans might be seen as actors in the wings of a stage considering the parts they will play and the interactions they will have, when they actually walk on to the stage.

As well as being a personal endeavour and responsibility, evolution is a collective journey. Many of the same conditions which apply to the individual also apply to the whole. The macrocosm and microcosm are interdependent reflections.

Guardian angels and guides

Each incarnating being draws towards itself a guardian angel who will accompany it from the moment of the decision to seek conception until its death. When each one of you dies, your guardian angel evolves to another point in the hierarchy of angelic beings. The guardian angel is not the same as a guide. Those whom you contact as true guides are of the human stream of consciousness and have reached a place where they may choose to serve on other planes and to help in building bridges between levels rather than reincarnating on earth. We have travelled a significant part of the journey which will enable us to have a full link with our own twin souls and then, so reunited, travel further in the journey to reunion with the Source.

Until the soul stem or strand has built up enough experience to be able to be active in the choice of what goes on in between lifetimes, the period after death is overseen by angels, by guides, by healers and helpers and by beings who have also travelled by the human stream of evolution and are known as Ascended Ones (sometimes as Ascended Masters, but this title is incorrect in more senses than that it comes from patriarchal thought forms. These Beings are complete in themselves, they are true androgynes). These Ascended Ones have chosen to keep a degree of personality and separateness in order to help forward both individual and collective evolution. They work closely with the angelic forces and act as guardians for humanity and the planet earth as well as holding contact with other life forms on other planets.

The 'between life' state

Thus when you die, you are welcomed on to the higher astral planes by healers. You are offered rest in colour healing temples and helped and cared for until the necessary adjustments from one plane of being to another are made. The transition through death is greatly helped if you have cultivated an open 'mental set' in your lifetime. If you have built up too strong a thought form about heaven being a rose-covered cottage in the country, then this is what it will be until your mental set expands. Of course such a thought form does not bring suffering in the after life, only limitation. Other thought forms of purgatory, no after life, no continuity of being, no hope of being forgiven, actually bring difficulty during the transition phase. Then angels, helpers and healers work very hard to 'rescue' such a person from their own bonds of belief. Those who commit suicide often have difficult thought forms to overcome. They are not exiled from other planes of existence or punished, but gently healed and helped to gain the strength to face whatever they need to face in order to continue their evolution.

Reviewing the life just lived

After the healing and resting period special workers help you to make an overview of the life which you have just lived on earth. This can be likened to an intensive psychotherapy. It can be painful and difficult to see the patterns and consequences of your behaviour from this wider perspective. There can, of course also be great pleasure as you notice the places where you were in harmony and caused light, love and healing to increase in the world.

The 'remedial zone'

After this, there is a reunification with your soul stem
or strand. Other guides, helpers and advisers aid in the
planning of the next stages of your evolution. The
personality you 'wore' in your lifetime will eventually
be reabsorbed into the soul stem. Until you are ready
for that to happen, you may spend some time in an
area of the astral plane, which I call the 'remedial
zone', where you can be active in your own self-
healing. Here you may meet loved ones from your
lifetime who have already passed over and have joyful
reunions with them. You may work with those with
whom you were in conflict or difficulty in your
lifetime, so resolving problems in this between-life
phase without having to take them into incarnation
again.

Eventually the reabsorption of the personality into
the soul stem will take place and then plans may be
made for another aspect to incarnate and take up the
baton of the evolutionary relay.

At a certain point it is no longer necessary to
reincarnate. Then the essence of your soul stem or
strand (not yet reunited with the twin stem or twin
strand) will become a more diffuse being than you
recognise in earth life, and will choose work to do on
these other planes. This may be healing, receiving
those who have recently 'passed over', work in the
remedial zone or supervision of life-reviews. It may be
wider work with energies, rhythms and patterns, in
close co-operation with the angelic hierarchies. It may
be work akin to architecture, helping to perfect
thought forms or to build the beautiful light temples
which exist on the etheric and astral planes. These
thought forms and light/sound temples will eventually
filter through to earth. Meanwhile they form a

'creativity bank' which can be tapped into when true earth inspiration is really flowing.

Being a guide is a form of work which can be chosen on our planes. We are usually attached to a group and, within that group, have a specific joint purpose. All guides, who concern themselves with the earth plane, are concerned with building bridges of communication so that those in incarnation do not feel exiled, isolated, abandoned, bewildered, without purpose or unsupported. We want to remind you that all life is a continuum; we want to help you in making the conditions of earth incarnation more gentle, less violent and more joyful.

Some guides, like myself, are communicators and teachers, others are more concerned with healing or with inspiring artists, writers and all who create. Each one of you has at least one guide watching over you and your life's journey. We welcome any opportunity to make this contact more conscious, but it can only be so at the point in your awareness where you will not expect us to live your lives for you or give your power away to us, thus abdicating responsibility for choice.

Soul families and groups

As well as being twin stems or bead strands, souls belong to families and groups, At the risk of 'mixing my metaphors' let me paint you another picture. First, imagine a tree, then the forest in which it stands, then many other forests of trees. Twigs, leaves and fruits which spring from the same branch are soul families. Branches on the same tree are soul groups, forests are wider soul groups. In life you meet those who are from the same branch as yourself and will often recognise them joyfully as true 'spiritual family'. (Genetic family is not necessarily spiritual family –

recognising this can often ease the build up of expectations within the genetic family.) You will also meet with those who are from your own tree and those who are of your wider group soul. Often so called 'difficult karma' comes from the efforts of soul family and group to mirror lessons for each other. The impulse of this mirroring comes from love and understanding and will have relevance to the joint evolution of the group.

You are never alone. You always have soul family and soul group contacts around you, joint work to be recognised and carried out, guides, and guardian angels as support. Sometimes you may seem to be living in conditions of isolation, or in alien territory. Even when the direct contacts are not there, try to sense all the subtle energetic forces of love and acceptance surrounding you.

Angels

Angels are from a different stream of consciousness. They will never incarnate, just as those of the human stream, contrary to much popular belief, will never become angels. There are different complex orders within the hierarchy of angels. The archangels are closest to the Source. They are great light beings whose task is one of guardianship in its widest sense. They also work to enable a greater connection between human minds and creativity, Divine inspiration and principle which flow constantly from the Source.

Angels are concerned with colour, fragrance, sacred geometry, sound and pattern within the universe and for helping to maintain essential balances.

Devas and elemental beings

Below the angels, in the same hierarchy, are the devas and elemental beings. Devas are 'shining spirits'. They guard trees, rocks, water sources, and contribute to the balancing of climatic conditions. They assist the angels in keeping a balance within the natural orders. Elementals work closely with the devas. They are the 'lowest' manifestation in the angelic/devic hierarchy. They are pure energy and may be perceived as dots of brilliant colour or light. Sometimes they imitate human form, hence the tradition of fairies, elves, goblins, undines, sylphs and salamanders or fire fairies.

Beings from other planets

Extra-terrestrials, or beings from other planets, also originate as sparks from the Source. They do not have an evolutionary structure as does the human stream of consciousness, for earth is the only planet of choice and free will. It is also the only planet of disease, but I shall speak more of this later.

Other planetary beings sometimes take on human form for a lifetime, in order to experience directly the conditions of earth. It is also possible for a human soul to send a personality spark to another planet, but there will always be essential differences in the original form of vitality between human beings and inter-planetary intelligences. Earth incarnation is concerned mostly with the earth element – the other elements: water, fire and air, are experienced in direct relationship to earth. On other planets the primary element of experience is different, thus changing all manner of form, possibility and awareness.

It is most correct to speak of beings from other

planets as 'intelligences'. They do not need bodies in the same way as you do on earth. Because their structure of existence is beyond your conception, when space beings endeavour to contact you they will assume a shape which approximates to an earth body. They also know that they need to materialise more solidly in order to survive earth's atmosphere, and so they seek ways of 'clothing' themselves more suitably. In doing this they hope to pierce through the veil of your more limited perceptions and thought forms, to make you aware of them and to seek to set up communication with you. When you open to their existence, you will begin to see them. Time and space barriers will be overcome and your total perception of the universe as whole, present and a part of your immediate experience will expand.

Enabling and allowing the communication of space beings is an essential part of movement into new dimensions. Your universe must expand. Other planetary intelligences can help you here – but, as I said before, do not make the mistake of seeing them as gods or saviours. Be open to the empowerment they can bring without giving your own power and integrity away.

Earth – the planet of choice

I have spoken previously of the earth as a planet of choice. Sometimes having to choose can seem to be too great a burden of responsibility, especially when you know that your ability to see the whole picture is limited. The original choice of humanity was for knowledge and experience rather than for innocence and protection. The end result will be empowerment. From a position of wisdom new choices may be made as to what is appropriate to be included in the range of human experience and what is better left aside.

With the faster communications which you now have, in your world, it is difficult for things to be covered or unknown. More of what is going on in the collective experience of humanity is available to the consciousness of more individuals than at any other time in the earth's history. The shadow side of human nature is revealed. This makes life in your times very difficult but it also means that you know with what you are dealing. The issue of choice is becoming more and more important. Earth, or Gaia herself, is forcing new decisions to be made. There must be a turnaround very soon. When enough human beings are ready to say, 'We need new boundaries and paradigms for human behaviour and the human condition and we are determined to take an active part in instigating these', then all the new dimensions and possibilities will be revealed. Negative thought forms which breed negative energy will be denied life-force and the behaviour patterns of greed, violence and self-seeking will cease to exist in just the way that a limb which is cut off from the blood supply will become useless, rot away and eventually drop off.

The shadow

That which is unacknowledged, unused, undefined or unfamiliar tends to merge into the shadow. The word 'shadow' cannot properly be used interchangeably with 'naughty', 'bad', 'violent' or 'evil'. I have noticed that it tends to be used frequently in growth circles when people are trying too hard to be 'mature', 'all-inclusive' and fashionably 'non-judgemental' about the difficult side of life and of other people's psyches.

The contents of the shadow can be powerfully creative. Fear denies the emergence of shadow material and so causes repression, not only of that which is truly frightening and destructive, but of much of the energy which, when released, can cause life to be more fertile and satisfying. If what is feared is pushed underground or into the unconscious, then it gains autonomy. If all shadows are allowed to surface they can be fully assessed. Decisions can be made about those which deserve life-force and those which need to be 'starved out'. Fear carries great energy and where it causes repression it gives power and vitality to the repressed object or drive, so that monsters indeed, are bred. Access to the creativity of the 'bright shadow' can only come when individuals become sufficiently empowered to recognise the destructive and deny it sustenance.

If the privilege of choice is going to be used wisely and well as part of the changes, then there has to be something of a shift in the area of 'woolly' non-judgementalism. Too much tolerance can breed inefficiency, low standards of behaviour and insecurity. The meaning of integrity can become obscured. Understanding what causes certain negative behaviours in fellow human beings and offering the right sort of loving rehabilitation is an essential part of compassion. Neither understanding nor compassion is about condoning behaviour which is destructive to the potential of the human race.

Fear and greed

The existence in your societies of such forces as war, crime, violence and even AIDS is mainly fuelled by fear or greed. The latter is certainly a monster of your present times which needs to be cut down to size – yet even this is a by-product of fear. Let me digress slightly in order to explain.

The Divine energies emanating from the Source eventually emerge, in the organisation of human societies, as archetypes. Some of these, currently need redefinition. The archetype of the warrior is a prime example. The pure warrior energy exists in order that clear boundaries may be defined and protected, particularly at a psychic level. The prime object of the true warrior is not to go out and attack for the sake of attacking, not to create a battlefield full of carnage, not to dissipate the life force of the peoples, but to maintain an agreed integrity. If this integrity comes under heavy threat then the warrior may have to use skill to prevent the menace from intruding. With alertness such incidents are contained with minimum bloodshed. They are perceived before they escalate. The skill of warriorship is spiritual and watchful, subtle and psychic as well as physical and direct. The warrior's aim is to protect standards and to nurture the people. The true warrior practises regularly the natural skills of defence, but knows that the happiest place for the sharpened sword is in its sheath. Attention to detail will prevent the sword's being unsheathed except for practice and honing.

Fear and greed increase the field of battle and fuel the need to have bigger and better weapons until those weapons themselves are a threat to the continuance of human existence.

The law of abundance

One of the basic laws of the universe is that of abundance. Few people in your times hold this in their belief system. Where this law is denied or transgressed the only result can be greed and crime. If you fear that there is not enough, then you will want to stockpile. If the result of stockpiling is that you are then seen as richer and more fortunate than others the negative side of power rears its ugly head and becomes associated with possessions or wealth. Maintaining power becomes a question of making sure that others have less than you. The energies escalate and have a 'knock-on' effect. Jealousy, intrigue, negative self-interest, violence, crime and fight for survival become the order of the day. No one trusts anyone else, all systems become corrupt.

There is enough of everything within the natural provision of earth for all to lead abundant lives. The distribution of resources has got out of hand. False hierarchies have been constructed on foundations of possessiveness, power and greed. You deny each other the divine right to 'be'.

In the pursuit of experience all these things had to happen, but now the negative side has escalated enough. The power of choice must be exerted to bring about a return to simplicity, non-possessiveness, abundance and love.

As systems break down, do not despair. With breakdown comes the opportunity for rebuilding. As you witness the collapse, concentrate on denying life-force to possessiveness and greed. Give the power of hope to respect, gentleness, abundance and love. Endeavour to practise these whenever you can in your immediate and daily lives.

Illness

Many illnesses are rich in symbolism. They mirror the lessons which have to be learned. This is true of AIDS. It should not be seen as a scourge meted out by an authoritarian God to be removed only when human

beings agree to conform once more and can therefore
be forgiven. It distresses us that such thinking exists.
The Source is Love. No caring force would deal out so
much pain. There is no virtue in suffering. No, AIDS
is illustrative of system breakdown. It is mirroring the
need for new awareness of causes and effects. AIDS is
not only the province of the individuals who contract it
but is symptomatic of issues which the whole of
humanity needs to address.

In a wider sense, degenerative disease enables
mutation. The vibratory rate of the human vehicle has
to change before new dimensions can be embraced.
Those who suffer diseases such as AIDS and cancer
play a part in enabling collective mutation. They may
have agreed to play this part, in consultation with their
higher selves and guides, before incarnation.

Dis-ease carries a wisdom within it. Total healing is
not accomplished by a return to a state of health which
has previously been known. Emergence from disease is
a transformation and renewal. Sickness shows that
something is out of balance. It is a signal of a need to
move on. Earth is the only planet where disease
enables conscious change. When the healing is
complete a new order will exist.

My cosmology does not include the belief that evil is
a competitive force opposing the good or Divine. Evil
is rather seen as a gross concentration of negative and
destructive energies which escalate and gain
autonomy. Eventually the concentration has to erupt.
It then manifests in negative power and regimes which
seek to control through fear. In your present time
many such regimes exist or have existed, in Nazi
Germany, Eastern Europe and the Far East. The good
news, however, is that as they are more clearly seen,
more and more sanctions, without recourse to war, are
being applied to those who are the leaders of them. An

evil human being is one who is possessed by the erupted and autonomous destructive energies. The state is always temporary or transient when seen against the whole backcloth of evolution. The essence of each human being is a clear flame. However it may be obscured, this flame will never be extinguished. Redemption will always come even though after many incarnations.

My cosmology assumes a belief in reincarnation. The journey of the soul in its relationship to earth takes many lifetimes. Learning and insight continues in the between-life phases. The concomitant of reincarnation is karma or the law of cause and effect. At the crudest level this is assumed to mean that an eye will be demanded for an eye and a tooth for a tooth. The true laws of karma are both more complex and more compassionate. They become very involved after soul families and groups have interacted with each other as well as with different soul groups and families for many incarnations.

Cause and effect; karma

Inevitably, when you make an action, you set ripples moving, as does a stone when it is thrown into still waters. You may not be aware of the extent of those ripples until you are able to see them from the perspective of the between-life state. When you become aware of the effects which you have caused (positive as well as negative), you take this information back to your soul stem or strand. Decisions are then made as to what needs to be done to bring about balance once more. Guides, helpers and karmic advisers will probably be consulted as well as other members of your soul family and group. The emphasis is on the best action which may be taken to improve the consciousness of your soul stem and enhance the experience of the group. There is no question of punishment, only of learning and expansion. Although springing from the same soul stem or strand it is a new personality which will take on the tasks to be completed and the new ground to be explored.

The concept of karma as punishment comes from the belief system which considers God to be a jealous God. Mind-set affects not only what happens in incarnation but the choices which are made between lifetimes and the imprint which the new personality brings into incarnation. Thus, the more the individual and collective mind-set is punishment-orientated, the more will the karmic conditions taken on be of a restrictive nature.

The issue of choice is probably at its most potent when making karmic decisions. At every stage the soul stem or strand may choose freely. Advisers are there, but they do not make the decisions. The incarnating bead or flower is seldom fully aware of the soul's purposes as it comes into incarnation. The urge to become conversant with these sets the incarnate being on the path of spiritual growth. Gradually the sphere of opportunity chosen by the higher self is understood and accepted. Limitations will be discovered within that sphere. These will be governed by such things as the choice of body, access to particular gifts, skills or intelligence, as well as the choice of parents, nationality, historical era and social environment.

Within the sphere of opportunity the incarnate being has free choice, or free will. Because the sphere has been circumscribed it is not possible to make 'wrong' choices in incarnation. (We know that many of you agonise over decisions!) Every decision leads to experience which furthers the evolution of the soul. Thus the incarnate personality is not without power or a certain freedom.

You do not need to see yourselves as victims of karma. The higher self is not bent on unnecessary restriction, neither is it opposed to contentment, fulfilment or abundance. Your soul group and its highest consciousness are all best served when you overcome obstacles and fulfil potential. The obstacles are there to make some karmic tasks more conscious. Too many people interpret seeming blockages as meaning that they are trapped by a karma which will hold them back from achievement or happiness. It is never wrong to strive to change your 'lot' in life. There is no reward for bending and surrendering too easily to limitation. Individual and collective beliefs about freedom and abundance are in urgent need of change.

Unfinished business

A particularly limiting thought form concerns 'unfinished business'. This label is often given to conflicts in relationships. A clash of wills and interest may make resolution or creative compromise impossible. When this happens it is better to declare that although the business seems unfinished, circumstances permit of nothing further being done. You can then release the situation, yourself and others involved so that you are all free to move on to other things. If you let unfinished business with another individual limit your movement and choices there is likely to be an even deeper karmic enmeshment in the long term. Karma is about learning through self-definition, integrity and increasing clarity. It is not a treadmill or life-sentence. Incarnation is not a form of exile.

It is demanding to live in your present times. Subtle changes in the substance of matter and the nature of time are gradually but constantly happening. One of the best ways in which to increase your vitality, health and stamina, as well as helping you to take a more conscious part in the changing vibrational patterns is to strengthen, invigorate and protect your aura. (Around each one of you there is an energy field or 'aura'. It is your own spectrum of colour and light.) The exercise below might be seen as 'psychic grooming'. It will also help you in dealing with atmospheric pollution of all kinds, including noise and intrusion.

I hope this overview may help you to a more coherent context in which to place some of my other comments.

Meditation to Help in Strengthening and Protecting Your Aura

You are going to breathe light and colour around your auric field. This will be healing, energising and protective. Seven bands of light and colour are breathed around the body from left to right, starting and ending at the feet, then seven more from back to front also starting and ending at the feet (see diagram on page 76).

The colour should be visualised or imagined as vibrant and translucent – like stained glass, when sunlight passes through it.

Eventually you can do this meditation in almost any position or situation, but first practise it standing if possible, or sitting on an upright chair.

The colours are: deep rose pink; amber; golden yellow; spring green; lapis lazuli blue; indigo; and deep violet.

Stand easily and comfortably. Pay attention to the balance of your head on your neck. Place your feet comfortably apart, do not tense your shoulders or lock your knees. Relax any tension in the lower part of your body and rock your pelvis a little until you have a relaxed stance. Before beginning to visualise the colours, pay attention to your breathing. Imagine a breath which starts underneath your feet on the in-breath and travels up the left side of your body to the crown of your head. Here you start the out-breath which goes down the right side of your body to the starting position under your feet. Practise these breaths until the rhythm is flowing easily.

Now, begin the light and colour breaths. Visualising rose pink light . . . breathe a band of this colour, up your left side, on the in-breath, keeping the colour band close to your physical body. At the crown of your head change to the out-breath and take the rose pink colour down the right side of your body, letting it join under your feet. Do the same with each colour in turn, moving slightly further out from your body as you breathe each new band, until you are surrounded with a rainbow of coloured light. Light and colour can interpenotrate with physical matter, so visualise the bands of light lying as evenly under your feet, as around the rest of your body.

Once you have established the spectrum of light around you in this direction, continue to breathe evenly. The next step is to breathe the light and colour bands around you from back to front. Again, you start under your feet, wth rose pink . . . breathe it up the back of your body to the crown of your head, on the in-breath and down the front of your body to join under your feet, on the out-breath. You end with violet, as before.

Having accomplished this part of the exercise continue to breathe evenly and let each band of colour expand and join around you until it forms an egg shape. Imagine a 'Russian doll' effect. You are in the centre, surrounded by seven eggs of light and colour. Feel strengthened, energised, protected and secure. Before you take up your normal tasks once more, visualise a silver egg of light enclosing the other seven. In this way, you take light and energy with you wherever you go, but are less vulnerable to any unwanted impingement from the outer world.

When you know this exercise well it is not always necessary to go through the complete breathing/visualisation — though it is a good meditative practice in itself. At any time when you feel vulnerable or in need of an energy boost, you can merely visualise the seven eggs of light and colour surrounding you, with the final egg of silver as a container for the energy and to help you in absorbing all the healing effect which light and colour can bring.

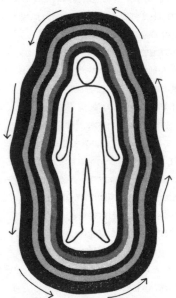

*Breathing colours
from left to right*

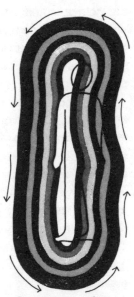

*Breathing colours
from back to front*

7

The Power of Healing

How can we use the power of healing to help ourselves? . . . Is there an acceptable philosophy of disease? . . . How can we tap into healing energy?

Gildas states that earth is the only planet on which part of our learning and evolution takes place through disease. The process of healing should not be seen as a return to a state of health previously known, but as a journey to new insight and maturity.

Symptom as Symbol

Disease is largely symbolic. If the word itself is split, it becomes dis-ease. We should take seriously those times when we are uneasy in our lives or bodies. The expectations others have of us and those we have of ourselves may cause us stress. The tendency is to 'give ourselves a good talking to', take a deep breath, call on our willpower and then carry on with the same old patterns. We do not easily see that such 'dis-ease' can eventually produce ill-health and sickness.

'Mind over matter' is an attitude to life which is often greatly admired even if frequently misunderstood. We endeavour to subjugate body and emotions to the discipline and directions of the mind. We are conditioned to, or filled with, expectations of what we 'ought' to be. Parents, teachers and society have an investment in moulding or forcing us into conformity. We are pressured into pursuing interests which others see as being 'good' for us. We must perform to a pre-set standard and generally become 'happy', 'normal', or 'well-adjusted'. Our minds learn to believe that the norm or expectation is right. We may turn ourselves inside out in order to please others and fulfil their ambitions for us. We desperately yearn for approval.

Finding the True Self

A gardener given some unlabelled but interesting-looking seeds which he has decided to plant will watch their growth carefully. He will assess their need for light or shade; more or less moisture; rich or less rich soil. As the plants grow the gardener will be interested to observe their progress and what sort of a plant they are becoming. Should they flower or fruit he will be delighted with the result. Whatever their shape, colour or size he will be content if they are healthy flourishing plants. He will let those which want to grow tall have support. He will see that the shorter, stumpier ones have enough light and ground space.

A gardener knows that a seed holds a certain blue-print or potential. It is useless to plant a tomato seed if you want to grow an oak tree; no amount of persuasion, tending, discipline or threats will make the seed change. If the conditions are not right for the seed, it will sicken and die.

Of course, the analogy between a seed and a human being cannot be pushed too far, but nevertheless it serves to set us thinking about the nature of disease. However much we may struggle to gain approval and to be what others ask of us, our feelings or emotions will eventually make it clear if we are a 'square peg in a round hole'. If feelings are ignored and the mind pushes us on, or entrenches us further, in areas where we cannot express the true self, the body will begin to collude. Instead of fighting to change our direction it may become passive.

It is more difficult to avoid the signals of the body than of the mind. If the body is ill, we cannot continue. If we ignore the messages of minor symptoms, they may develop into something more major or we may have an accident. Pain is an example here. It is nature's way of signalling when something is wrong. If we kill the pain with pills, before diagnosis, we are destroying the messengers carrying the message and are in danger of leaving the real cause of the trouble undetected and untreated. If we do not examine our life-style, a really serious illness or breakdown may develop. Heart attacks and life-threatening illnesses force us to consider our quality of life. If we survive, life changes may be made which enable more of the true self to shine through.

Instead of seeing disease as an attacker or a monster on the path, we should consider the symbolic wisdom which it encompasses. Certainly in its earlier stages symptoms carry warnings. They are potential friends or allies. Every symptom bears a different message. Although there may be a common thread in the message which a particular group of symptoms carries, the total communication to the individual manifesting such symptoms is unique and personal. Lists suggesting symbolic meanings for symptoms should be used only as a guide to further personal insight. To be told that if you have trouble with your gall bladder you are unconsciously bitter, may bring insight to some, but guilt and self-recrimination to others. Bitterness (because of the gall) must certainly be considered by those with weakness in this area but a less accusatory, categorical or judgemental way of opening the exploration may be to ask: 'What is the bitter pill which life has asked me to

swallow? Do I need to continue to do so? Is there something
I might change to my own advantage?'

Self Responsibility

In 'alternative medicine' circles there is an attitude about
self responsibility which can all too easily add the burden of
guilt to that of disease. Regarding symptom as symbol
should not be a way of saying: 'It's really all your fault.
You've done this to yourself, so what are you going to do
about it now?' Rather, the exploration of symptom as
symbol should be exciting, exploring the symbol as a key to
what may be required to release the potential of the true
self.

To consider the symbology of the many symptoms which
we humans can manifest is beyond the scope of this book.
The points to consider are: (a) disease and symptoms may
be allies rather than enemies; (b) there is often a greater
wisdom within the 'sick-self' than in the 'conditioned
well-self'.

This approach can lead us to see that there is a potent
natural force using each human being to release a unique
and powerful potential. When the individual achieves this,
the whole of humanity will do so too. Not only the general
power of healing, but the power of self-healing will enable
humanity to transform.

Healing Power

If there is, as Gildas and other guides urge us to believe, a
breathtakingly beautiful blueprint for the universe, then it
follows that there is a universally available source of healing
power.

We can tap into this source of healing in order to realise

our true potential; but we cannot use it nor can it be harnessed on our behalf by a healer, until we have learned the reasons which caused the disease to manifest. It is unlikely that we will be healed sufficiently to go on driving ourselves relentlessly on some treadmill if our bodies and emotions know that we would be more fulfilled in crofting, helping in the 'third world' or merely 'being' rather than striving and doing.

Body and emotions are strong and direct in their communication. Economics and false expectations do not matter to them. If we are out of balance or thwarting our true talents they will collude to warn us time and again. If the warning is unheeded then breakdown or chronic illness is likely to result.

Though chronic illness often cuts across our conditioned ambitions it may also obtain hidden 'benefits' which we could not allow ourselves to ask for, or have, without being ill. Understanding these benefits may be a complex task. If it is undertaken, choice, even from within a sick body, may become available again, where formerly it seemed blocked.

When the power of healing is invoked, it causes change. The 'miracle cure' may not be possible but if we allow ourselves to embrace change other sorts of miracles happen. We find or accept new opportunities in directions undreamt of before.

Some illness can be karmic, though less often than many seem to believe. Sometimes there is a sacrificial element. Disease is 'taken on' by an individual or group in order to teach others compassion, to change a collective belief system, or as stated by Gildas, in the last chapter, to enable mutational change to happen.

Through disease there may be transformation, but it is not necessarily seen by the guides as an ideal way of learning. When we overcome the powerful myth that we *need* to suffer in order to learn, then disease will recede. When we recognise that our true selves are welcome and revise our expectations then disease as a wise messenger will be redundant.

Here are some direct words form Gildas about healing:

GILDAS

The ability to tap into the power of healing is gradually being re-learned. Complete healing must do more than remove or relieve symptoms. You must expect it to be a journey – and one in which death is not seen as 'failure'. The nature of being is eternal and death, in its natural rhythm, is an opening to a new and exciting stage.

More and more people want to train or explore the natural ability to heal. They are ready and willing to accompany others on their healing journey. To some extent this is a revival of the skills known to priests and priestesses in some ancient civilisations. The power of a healer to help is limited if you expect their ministrations to act magically, swiftly, more conveniently and with less side effects than a toxic allopathic drug. Healing must be seen as a holistic and co-operative experience, requiring a great deal of insight and commitment to change.

Healers must not be seen or expected to be perfect. They should be sufficiently open to their own journey to have travelled some distance, but they will most usually be fellow travellers – not authoritarians. In such companionship there is more equality, and the disablement of 'handing over power', which is at the basis of so much disease, can be avoided.

Harnessing healing energy

To some extent you can all harness healing energy for yourselves and others. Open up to that universal flow which carries perfection within it! See it as a golden or rainbow light. Visualise it around yourself or another person, ask for healing to happen – and it will. Just remember that the healing will necessarily be limited until you are open to change and the birth of your true self.

When you commit to your own healing journey you help the whole of humanity. The individual and the collective can never be separated. You repeatedly ask how you can help and your concern is precious to us. Of course some of you will know that you must help in a more dramatic or active way – but self-healing acts for the whole and is not necessarily circumscribed or selfish.

Being prepared for perfection

One question which I would ask you is: 'Are you prepared for perfection?' When you are, then it will happen – but until enough individuals believe this to be possible on earth, it will be blocked, because it is not sufficiently present in the belief system. What you believe to be impossible usually is. Healing is both complex and simple. What you must work at is believing that the power and possibility is there. You do not have to believe in the healers or their power – just that healing is natural and that health, wholeness and joy are allowed. When the changes are fully established, there will no longer be the necessity for disease or ageing beyond the point of optimum bodily strength, beauty and vitality. You will be able to live out your earth span in the best possible physical condition.

This perfection of form and the sustainment of it for the life-span can only come about when there is an acceptance that life on earth will always have a limited, though rhythmic span. When the time comes to go to other levels, to experience other aspects of life, then you will leave with dignity. Your loved ones will not grieve in the same way, because communication between the planes will be easy and immediate. You will only have to think of a loved one to be in their presence.

Though it is good and right that this freedom from disease should come, in the present years which immediately precede change or breakthrough, collectively you have the last opportunity to recognise the wisdom of disease, and to bring to a conscious end the purpose which it has served.

A Healing Meditation

This meditation can be used for self-healing or you can visualise someone else in the healing light.

Make sure that you are not going to be disturbed. If possible light a candle and dedicate it to your healing. Sit or lie in a comfortable, symmetrical position and become aware of the rhythm of your breathing ... Within the breath rhythm become aware of your heart centre or chakra. (This is on a level with your physical heart but in the centre of your body — it can open and close like a flower — see page 114) ... Feel the heart chakra's petals opening, allowing the heart energy to flow ...

Travel on the heart breath into your inner space and imagine yourself walking along a wooded pathway ... The ground is soft under your feet and the fragrance of leaf mould is around you ... sun is dappling through the trees and you can hear the sound of water ... Soon you see a busily babbling stream, through the trees and you walk towards it . . . You decide to follow the stream, walking in the direction from which it is flowing . . . Soon you come out of the wood and the ground is drier and quite stony . . . You are going gently uphill . . . Now there are some bigger rocks around and you become aware of a waterfall somewhere near . . . You come upon the waterfall rather suddenly . . . It is splashing down from some higher rocks into a natural pool, from which the stream runs . . . the sun is shining and a misty spray rises from the water . . . In the sunlight, the spray is full of rainbows . . .

You find a smooth rock, which has been warmed by the sun . . . As you sit on it, you realise that you are being bathed in rainbow healing light . . . Sit for a while and let the light flow over and into you . . . Feel it going to any place where there is pain or unease . . . Feel the vitality which it brings . . . When you feel ready to do so, you will get up and make your way back alongside the stream to the woody path where this journey began . . . Before you leave the place of the waterfall, wash your hands and perhaps drink from the clear water in the pool . . . In the depths of the pool there may be a gift for you . . . a symbol to help you on your healing path . . .

After your return to the wooded path, become aware of the rhythm of your breathing and of your heart centre . . . Enter the outer world once more . . . blow out your candle . . . let the flower of your heart centre close in a little . . . Visualise a cross of light in a circle of light as a blessing over it.

8

Contacting Our Guides

We all have guides but how can we contact them? . . . What does their presence mean in our lives? . . . How can we learn to recognise how our lives have been guided? . . . How can we best prepare for meeting our guides?

In Chapter 6 Gildas speaks of soul groups, soul families, guides, helpers and guardian angels. He reminds us that we are never really alone either *horizontally* or *vertically*. Somewhere in incarnation, at the same time as ourselves, there will be other members of our soul family, while we are also surrounded by 'invisible' presences to whom our interests are dear. As well as taking on incarnation for our own evolution, in some sense we are ambassadors for the soul group. All the support we can conceivably need is available.

If we review our present lifetime, certain landmarks and turning points will clearly emerge. We were perhaps travelling in a certain direction – and may even have been rather set on it – but something happened which forced us to change. Maybe a new opportunity opened up before us or a door closed very firmly in front of us making us take stock and change direction. Where doors have been slammed in our faces, we may still bear resentment and disappointment. Until we recognise that we have a certain destiny (within which choice and scope are available), we may feel that we have been guided by knocks on the head and kicks from behind. Until we achieve some sense of alignment with an overall purpose in our lives, we may be too limited by the conditioning of society, parents and teachers. We may be slavishly following the mundane expectations of others – moulding ourselves to become what they expect of us. At least any pathway mapped out by our higher selves takes into account our true essence and our whole evolution.

Preparing to Meet Your Guide

When we have garnered a sense of alignment with our higher selves we may not readily know the direction to take at each of life's crossroads but we will be more open to making creative choices and taking responsibility for them. We will be more able to cope with the disappointments of ambitious or non-ambitious outer influences as we follow our own conditioning which has shaped us and know how much of it we wish to reject.

If you decide to make a life review, take pencil, paper and crayons and arrange to spend an hour or so in which you can quietly reflect. Arrange to be free of any likely outer disturbance, switch off the phone and be prepared to ignore the doorbell.

Life often follows approximately seven-year cycles or phases. Begin with where you are now. Consider your blessings, your difficulties and those things you would like to change. Record these and maybe make some drawings. Ask yourself whether there are any key words which summarise your feelings and needs. Cast your mind back over the previous seven-year span. Dwell on anything which readily comes to mind, then let it go and see whether other memories surface. Do not strive to remember overmuch. Trust your psyche – it will give you what is necessary. Even if it seems that all the material you are looking at is well known and familiar there will be some reason why you should be considering it again at this time. If you try to force hidden memories to emerge, you will achieve the opposite effect. If you are gentle with yourself and accept that which comes readily, your psyche will reveal more and more in its own time.

You need to build up trust between your conscious self and your wounded, vulnerable or hidden parts. Again make notes, write down key words and maybe do some drawing. Go right back through your entire life in this way, taking seven-year periods and making notes. End with your birth, write down things you have been told about your entry into the world, but also endeavour to get in touch with your feelings about how it was for you to come into incarnation into the family and circumstances you chose. Maybe meditate a little about this and ask for a symbol or image.

When you read through your life review, trends and signals and evidence of some kind of guidance will emerge. You may feel angry with your guides or guardian angel that you have not been more protected or better informed. It is important to recognise and deal with this anger before you can move forward into contact with a guide. Remember that we often give our guardian angels, in particular, quite a rough time. Do not forget they have to allow us our freedom, even if we insist on walking along the edge of a sheer and crumbling cliff. They may only be able to step in at the last moment to prevent total disaster. They must then stand by and see whether we have learned from experience or whether we will persist in the same patterns until we are thoroughly exhausted or battered by life.

Releasing Expectations

It is essential to get beyond the expectation that our guides and angels *ought* to be looking after us, telling us which way to go, which choices to make, who our true-self really is or what it requires. It may seem paradoxical, but guides will not help us to a really conscious contact while we maintain any expectation that they will make all our choices for us and run ahead of us to smooth our paths. We must take responsibility for ourselves. Guides have lived out their lives and it is not their task to live ours for us.

The Advantages of Guidance

We might well ask: 'If we have to release any expectations of our guides to this extent, is there really any advantage in contacting them?'

As I have already explained, I have been aware of Gildas' presence since early childhood. Outer conditioning and disapproval made me push him and my other subtle perceptions away with nearly disastrous results. When I denied my other vision, the outer world began to fade and during my teenage years I was threatened with blindness. At nineteen I was guided by a series of metaphysical knocks on the head and kicks from behind to the place where I would meet someone in the outer world who could help me to value all my perceptions. My eyesight stabilised and Gildas began to communicate through me and take an active part in my inner guidance and training.

Today, thirty-six years later, I have a wonderfully creative and trusting working partnership with Gildas. I have accepted the life-style which this necessitates. The teenage threat of blindness made me fully aware of my options. I believe that I could have made other choices without paying the price of my eyesight. I just had to know more clearly what each choice involved. I was not forced or coerced into the work I do today, or the continuing relationship with Gildas. Yet sometimes I have been very angry with myself, my higher self, Gildas and 'God'. Sacrifices of a kind have undoubtedly been demanded of me but there have been a lot of 'perks' along the way.

Gildas has never made decisions for me. He has been there as a trusted friend and adviser . . . but the choices have been mine. (Perhaps it is my innate stubbornness which has made our relationship a successful one!) In all my choices he has been non-judgemental and supportive. He has helped me to pick up the pieces when things have gone 'wrong'. In addition, he has shared his wider perspective and viewpoint. He has helped me and others to find meaning when all seems hopelessly jumbled, fated or without hope. He has taught me about healing and enabled me to teach others. Need I say more about the advantages of guidance?

It is not necessary to have a natural facility for extended perception in order to contact a guide. Sensitivity is more easily developed than may be supposed. Each guide will find a way of establishing a bridge of communication when the time is right and when we signal that we are willing for this bridge to be built. My contact with Gildas which has grown very direct and fluent over the years, should not be taken as a model. The communication of each guide is unique and personal. Finding the right mode of communication can be exciting; a voyage of exploration.

Gildas communicates in words which I receive as a kind of dictation. Other guides give key words, symbols or images which then have to be interpreted. Some communication is more indirect. It may depend on synchronicity – you pick up the right book at the right time; meet the right person at the right time; find yourself in the right place at the right time.

Making Regular Times

All communication with guides is enhanced if you make regular time for it. This does not have to be in a highly disciplined way. When you have a half-hour to spare, sit down with a notebook and record the questions you want to ask or the things you want to tell your guide. Do a meditation, such as one of those at the end of this chapter and then await results. Do not expect instant communication. Making the connection and finding out the form guidance will take for you, requires time, patience and the clearing away of expectations.

If you are tied to a particular expectation about the nature of your guide or what form the meeting might take then you will limit your opportunities. It is better to remain openly expectant – confident that conscious contact with guidance can be made, but open to whatever pattern it may take.

Having recommended this condition of 'open expectation', some qualification of openness is necessary. There are several different levels on the astral planes, where meetings with discarnates take place. Usually the only guides with whom it is advisable to seek contact are those who have completed many incarnations and are now choosing to serve the soul group and the cause of humanity from the higher astral plane (see page 120).

The lower levels of the astral plane and parts of the etheric are areas where lower thought forms or entities may be encountered. Other layers, or areas of the astral plane are those to which we go, initially after the death of the body. Sometimes relatives or friends who have recently 'passed over' make contact with those still in incarnation, through dreams, insistent thoughts or perhaps through a 'medium'. It has to be said that only occasionally is someone who has recently died qualified to be a guide. Anyone still attached to their lifetime personality is unlikely to have either the wide experience of the other planes, or the detachment to help us in the same way as can the true guides. There is a strange tendency in us to assume that all who have died, suddenly become wise. We would rarely have listened to, let alone acted upon, Aunt Lucy's advice. Yet, if we are told three weeks after her death, that she wants to organise our lives from 'beyond the veil', there is a strong temptation to allow her to do so. We really do find choice and responsibility a burden!

Making Our Part of the Journey

If we long to meet our true guides, the operative word is 'meet'. This implies travelling our part of the distance to a rendezvous. It is not enough to be receptive and say: 'I am willing to meet my guide just as soon as he/she chooses to come to me.' The reasons for having to make some effort towards a meeting are not moralistic or judgemental. They are reasons of safety. The higher guides meet us at a higher level of consciousness mainly for our own protection. In an emergency they will penetrate into our everyday level of density in order to help us. If they always did this then we would lose the opportunity to develop our fine perceptions and might be vulnerable to lower entities who, at best are manipulative or mischievous and, at worst, are malign and destructive.

Natural Sensitivity

We are often unaware of the natural facility we already possess for being able to enter altered states of consciousness and develop a fine discrimination required in receiving and evaluating guidance. Each incarnate human being experiences a number of different states of consciousness during the natural course of each day. We have periods or phases of being wide awake and full of physical energy, mentally alert, surging with creativity, relaxed, tense, receptive, out-going, inwardly reflective, dreamy and detached – and so on. It is a relatively small step, requiring a minimum of training, to be able to use some of these states at will. Very little esoteric knowledge is required. While a knowledge of chakras and the steps in energy which they represent may be helpful, it does not have to be extensive. It is enough to know that there are eight main subtle energy centres interpenetrating with the physical body and extending into the auric field. For purposes of attunement these centres can become a focus for raising and refining energies, or, in other words, for making our part of the journey to the place where we may meet our guides.

Chakras

The diagram on page 94 shows how the chakras relate to, and interpenetrate with, the physical body. Starting at the chakra in the perineum area, they are named, in ascending order: the root; the sacral; the solar plexus; the heart; the throat; the alter major; the brow; the crown. The first exercise at the end of this chapter will enable you to use these energy steps to attain that level at which you are most receptive to guidance communication, and any meeting with your guide is safe. (See the Glossary for more about chakras.)

Before handing over to Gildas, I should like to consider some common questions about guides and guidance.

How many guides is any one person likely to have?

In the first instance it is better to concentrate on meeting one guide. Later, another may appear, perhaps to advise on

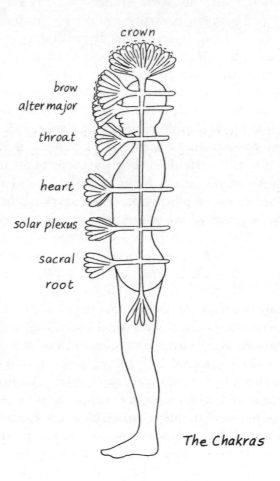

brow
alter major

throat

heart

solar plexus

sacral

root

crown

The Chakras

different kinds of issues. Sometimes one guide leaves after communicating for a while and another appears. Having many guides, except for very special reasons or where the individual had a lot of experience in this field, would make me concerned. I should want to discover whether there was an unwise degree of openness or lack of discrimination.

Are all guides masculine?

Guides usually manifest in the gender which is their true or original essence. It does seem that there is a preponderance of male teaching guides, but those more concerned with healing are often feminine.

How can I know what is guidance and what is a part of myself? Are they perhaps one and the same?

Gildas is quite separate from me in identity. Over the years, various people have suggested that he is my higher self, my inner wise being or my animus. In some senses it does not really matter. Whatever it is seems to say things which are helpful, bring love and hope and offer a different perspective. I can only say what I experience and what I have observed when working to help others develop guidance.

We all have an inner wise part. Somewhat paradoxically when this part is known and active we can most easily meet with a true discarnate guide and monitor that meeting with discernment. We all have a higher self, which is that stem or strand from which our incarnate personality springs. Psychologists have demonstrated that within the psyche we are legion, with sub-personalities, manifestations of archetypes and animus or anima, all part of the merry band. But there is a complete difference of energy in meetings with the inner parts or even the higher self and in meeting with a discarnate guide or other entity. When getting to know the parts which are essentially aspects of our psyche and soul we may marvel at our diversity or richness. At the same time we grow to accept them as constituents of the Self. They appear to us, we recognise and own them, change or transform them and when we have integrated them know that we have performed a great work of Individuation.

With discarnate guides there comes a moment when we

recognise that not only are we seeing them, but they are seeing us. A very exciting encounter is taking place between discrete beings, revealing all manner of vital and creative potential.

Let Gildas tell us more from his perspective:

GILDAS

Recognising your guide

A question which I am frequently asked is: 'Who is my guide?' Perhaps surprisingly this is a difficult question to answer specifically. As guides we have a much more diffuse being or essence. Our 'bodies' are made up of subtle energy and light and colour. We are no longer limited by some of the restrictions of personality. We have incorporated and transcended most of our incarnate experience.

When we make contact with you, we try, at least in the initial stages, to find a link which will help you to recognise us. Usually you and the one who is now your guide will have met in a past incarnation. Sometimes several such meetings will have taken place.

Thus, in order to help you recognise us, we will 'clothe' ourselves in such a way as to touch off any link we can find. Ruth and I had shared a past monastic connection with France, so that one of the ways in which I could come close to her was in the identity of a monk, which is the one I had in my last earth life in fourteenth-century France. I am not now limited by this identity, but assuming it again enables me to make the kind of close and tender contact with your world which we seek. A completely disembodied essence is too ethereal or fragile for initial contact. We know that you more easily relate to a personality.

There are a number of different 'garments' which we might choose in order to better enable our contact with you. Yet on this side of life we do not meet each other as monks, Native American Indians, Tibetans, nuns, Chinese ... We know each other's energy bodies and colours and our communication is more direct, without the need for words and language. We communicate mind to mind and thought to thought.

Those seeking to know the identity of their guide may be puzzled if they consult mediums or sensitives who each describe someone different. When the medium makes contact with the stem or strand of the soul all the personality 'garments' are in evidence. Thus differences are not usually descriptive of disparate essences but occur because there are many possible manifestations of the same essence.

All that is required for the training of your sensitivities and the raising of your consciousness is a degree of commitment, insight and self-determination. It is far better to be patient and seek your own meeting with your guide than to rely on what you are told by sensitives or their communicators. When you make your own journey, you build up a body of experience. When your efforts result in connection with your guide, you can more easily accept it as genuine, knowing that your mind and imagination have not been influenced by anything you have been told.

Your guide will always be a member of your soul group. As guides we also belong to other groups with special concerns. When we link with you we help in improving the communication between different planes and levels of being. We may invite you to become more involved in working with us. Such a commitment might necessitate changes in your outer life. We have observed that the fear of your life being dramatically changed by contact with a guide can be an obstacle which holds you back from making the journey towards us. If you feel blocked in your access to guidance check your feelings and motives. Remember that you always have choice. We may offer you opportunities but we never impinge, drive or insist. You can enjoy guidance at what ever level you wish. We will not make insistent demands upon you.

Seek advice from a spiritual organisation or a Transpersonal Counsellor if you ever feel driven or intruded upon by a guide. Either a demanding subpersonality is 'colouring' the connection or there is some other factor in the relationship between you and your guide which requires clarifying.

We seek an open and gentle contact with you. We do not want to dominate your life or make your choices and decisions for you. If you expect this you make it difficult for us to come close. We have no choice but to wait a while, until you are more centred and self-determined.

Initiating contact with your guide

One of the best ways in which to initiate contact with your guide is to act 'as if' the link is there. Get a beautiful notebook. Write down not only the things which you wish to ask of us, but the things you would tell to an intimate friend. Do not assume that we can see every part of you. We long for your dialogue and for you to receive ours. Once you start your 'guide book' set time aside on a regular basis, not only to write more, but to look at what you have written previously. Then consider whether any of the questions you were asking have been answered. Study the form in which the answer came. In this way you will build a frame of reference and begin to have a greater awareness of the many different ways in which guidance can be communicated.

When you have established your 'guide book' and have recognised some of the ways in which guidance comes to you, consider your preferences, so that you can strengthen our guidance connection.

If you want to receive writings from your guide and feel this to be compatible for you, set aside a regular time for free writing. Become quiet and centred. Consider the issues on which you would like guidance. Attune to your brow chakra (see the exercise at the end of this chapter) and write down any thoughts or information which come into your awareness. Alternatively you might speak words and sentences into a tape recorder.

If you prefer images and symbols, again make time to be receptive. Write down descriptions of what you see, or of symbols which are described to you, or use drawing as a means to enhance this form of communication. In the ensuing days reflect on what you have received. Gradually you will learn to interpret this form of guidance, but remember that a symbol is always a rich gift. It will work for you at a deep level, even though you may not fully understand it mentally or intellectually.

Signs that your guide is a true guide

Try to be alert to the quality of your interaction with your guide. When you are attuned to a true guide, you will receive a subtle training in how to improve your own sensitivity, and thus the contact.

Seek advice if your guide is judgemental or over-directive. You should have the sense of a gentle, loving presence, who will accept you as you are, gently encourage you to build on your strengths, and accept your weaknesses. Your guide's presence should never interfere overmuch with your outer life and commitments unless you choose to let it do so. We are out of touch with your time dimension and you may have to educate us. Never be afraid to set your own pace and say when the time is not right. True guides respect you and your space. Gradually we will come as close to you as you wish, but you should feel in command. Never be a 'puppet' for a discarnate communicator.

The 'vibrational frequency' of your guide's presence should be a joy and should energise you. Again, I would ask you to seek advice if you feel drained by any experience of guidance. In the widest possible sense everything about your guide should 'smell' good and give you a 'lift', as does a beautiful fragrance.

When you check the quality of any communication you receive, particularly if it is in words, you may say inwardly: 'I think I knew this already. Is it really a guide, or am I just speaking wisely to myself?' This is a good sign. We endeavour to speak through the wise part of yourselves. The guidance which we give should not be startling, uncomfortable, or over-confrontational. Gentleness, empathy, compassion and progressive revelation are our key words. You will gradually recognise a particular 'tone' to the words which come from your guide. There may be a turn of phrase which you would not normally use or some other form of expression, uncharacteristic to you. On the whole, guides will not speak to you in archaic language. We use your known vocabulary and language. Our aim is to have a natural, easy, companionably loving relationship with you and to strengthen the bridges of light between the planes.

As the changes take place, and matter refines, it will become easier for us to help you to build the necessary bridge of contact. We can then guide and advise you, constantly show you the wider perspective and encourage you to keep your imagination and mind-set supple and open.

There will always be some people who will work more closely with us and who will channel our teachings to wider groups, but as much individual and personal contact as possible is important to us in our role in enabling the Golden Age to manifest. Devoting time to nurturing a contact with your guide is a way in which you can help yourself and speed and expedite the vertical communication which is so essential in the coming years.

Meditative Exercise for Raising Consciousness through the Chakras in Preparing to Meet Your Guide

Look at the diagram on page 94 and be aware of where the chakras lie in relationship to your physical body.

When you are ready to begin, sit on a reasonably upright chair, or in a lotus or cross-legged position on the floor. Make sure that your spine is straight and your head comfortably balanced on your neck. Become aware of the rhythm of your breathing and let the breath help you to become calm and peaceful.

Use your breathing to help you to focus your attention into the area of your root chakra. When you can sense its energy, visualise a cross of light in a circle of light as a blessing resting over its petals. Now, counting an in-breath and the following out-breath as one 'breath step', take six 'breath-steps' to bring your attention into your sacral chakra. As soon as you are aware of this energy centre, put the cross of light in a circle of light over it and take six breath-steps to the solar plexus. Become aware of the solar plexus, bless it with the cross of light in the circle of light and move, by six breath-steps to your heart chakra. The crosses and circles of light prevent energy 'loop backs' into the lower chakras.

From the heart onwards continue to bring your attention into each chakra in turn, but do not use the light symbol as before. Go right up to your crown chakra and then take six breath-steps down again to your brow. Hold your attention here. If your attention wanders, just bring it back calmly to this point. Be peaceful. Hold in your mind any issues on which you wish to receive guidance. Have an open expectation of meeting with your guide and of knowing your guide's name, but try not to strain for a particular type of experience or result. Stay at this point for ten to fifteen minutes.

When you are ready to finish, take six breath-steps up to your crown chakra. Bless your crown chakra with a cross of light in a circle of light. Take six breath-steps down to your brow and bless your brow chakra. Continue down to your alter major, your throat and your heart, blessing each one in turn with the light symbol. Go down through the solar plexus and the sacral centre to the root. Re-bless each of these centres with the light symbol. Put your feet firmly on the ground and surround yourself with a cloak of white light with a hood. In this way you take light with you, wherever you go, without being open and vulnerable.

Visual Meditative Exercise to Help in Meeting Your Guide Safely

This visualisation accomplishes the same purpose of raising the energies as the preceding exercise. It will appeal more to those who enjoy guided visualisation.

Make sure that you will be undisturbed. Sit or lie comfortably, with your body in a balanced and symmetrical position . . . become aware of the rhythm of your breathing . . . Bring the breath rhythm into your heart centre, so that the petals of your heart chakra open and your heart energy flows strongly . . . On the heart breath, travel into your inner space . . . and find yourself in a meadow . . . Take the opportunity of being in the meadow to enjoy your inner senses . . . See the objects and the colours . . . Hear the sounds . . . Feel the textures . . . Smell the fragrances . . . Taste the tastes . . . Beyond the meadow you can see a mountain and the pathway which leads to it . . . Near the top of the mountain there is an interesting-looking plateau . . . You are going to journey there and you prepare to set out . . .

As you go, be aware of the landscape through which you pass . . . When you come to the plateau, take some time to look around and explore . . . You will find a source of water here, from which to refresh yourself . . . When you are ready, find a comfortable, sheltered, warm place in which to sit . . . Reflect on the issues on which you would like to receive guidance — the questions you would like to ask . . . Wait with open expectation and receptivity . . . You may meet your guide here, sense a presence, or receive direct messages or symbols . . . You may only receive a sense of peace and relaxation . . . appreciate whatever it is you experience . . .

After 15 – 20 minutes make the journey back to the meadow in your own time . . . From the meadow become aware of the breath in your heart centre . . . your body . . . your outer surroundings . . . Put your feet firmly on the floor and breathe the cloak of light with its hood right around you, before connecting again with your everyday activities.

9

In Summary

and Conclusion

The guide's view of the future summarised . . . Should hope be our key-word? . . . How soon will our bodies change? . . . Will matter be the same? . . . Is 'God' dead? . . . Will we all be in contact with guides, angels and other planets?

GILDAS

The main key-note of our messages to you will always be that of love, but closely alongside it goes hope. You are facing difficult times now, but try not to dwell on disaster. We see breakthrough as imminent. You may feel that there is still far to go, but the understanding which enables change comes between one breath and the next. The changes of which we speak do not depend on technological advances. A change in dimension is a change in perception. The preparatory work is almost over, you are immersed in it now. When a mountain climber is almost at the top of the last cliff face he dare not look behind, for fear of vertigo or loss of perspective. He cannot yet see the view from the top. All that is there is sheer cliff face and the exhaustion which will suddenly drop away as the goal is reached. You are on that final cliff face. Soon, new ground will be under your feet, the new outlook visible.

I always find it difficult to give you a time – lest that time should run out and cause you to lose trust in the future or to doubt the bridge between the planes. However, I estimate that you will be more aware of the nature of the breakthrough by 2020 and that there will be positive changes of a nature which is beyond your present most optimistic imagination by 2050.

Your bodies are already in the process of change. Their substance is being refined as a part of the journey into the fifth dimension. There is a gradual but dramatic and intense infusion of light taking place, which is changing the constitution of matter and making changes possible, which, as yet, are only on the periphery of your finite vision.

Your bodies are changing through some of the very experiences which, at present, appear to you as negative. The hole in the ozone layer is causing stronger light and heat to flow through into earth's atmosphere. Global warming appears to be dangerous but it too is playing its part in change. Difficult illnesses such as AIDS or cancer enable mutation. I am not saying that you should endeavour to accelerate any of these things, but it is important to view them symbolically and creatively, to be less afraid of what is happening and to maintain hope.

Your bodies *are* matter. Just as they are changing so is all substance. In being refined and filled with light, it is becoming less dense and heavy, more supple and subtle, more buoyant and less bound by limitations of all kinds.

The perception of 'God' as a masculine, jealous, judgemental, parent figure is dying indeed. Such a death needs to be accelerated and celebrated. You have, for too long, been bound by a sense of sin and laboured in your ability to rejoice. You tend to see incarnation on earth as a form of exile or as punishment for 'original sin'. As the old understanding of 'God' dies the True Source of Unconditional Love can be born. The symbol for this is the yin and the yang – within its apparent simplicity all manner of Divine Principles are revealed, for all peoples, all faiths, all religions.

Yes, you will all be in contact with guides, angels and other planets. The quality of the fifth dimension will enable this. Barriers of time and space and some of the limitations of the finite mind will be overcome. The new experience is effortless and graceful. Now, the nature of matter makes your lives ponderous and cumbersome. The breakthrough, or quantum leap in consciousness, will change all this. The new constitution of matter will mean that anything which is created will manifest quickly without recourse to the clumsiness of technology. Earth as the plane of matter will still be important, because manifestation is a divine principle. A particular density of form only exists on earth. Although the matter which enables that form will be different it will still be a unique and necessary constituent within the totality of expression which is the universe.

Our contact with you will be easier and closer. This prospect delights and excites us. When you become aware of some of the previously unseen patterns which govern the universe, you will be free to travel vertically as well as horizontally – to other planes as well as over the surface of earth. Your bodies will be light and altered states of consciousness more easily accesssible. You will lose your sense of loneliness and exile and know the joys of co-creativity.

Interplanetary travel

Beings from other planets will be able to share their experiences with you and you will be able to visit their worlds. All created beings will work together, in harmony and consciousness, to realise potentials within the universe which cannot be fully tapped until there is a greater communication between all intelligences.

Your guardian angels will be your constant companions. The archangelic beings will have a clear part in your daily lives.

The Golden Age really is golden in colour. You can help it to manifest by visualising golden light pouring into matter and being absorbed by it until it also emits a golden glow. Include your bodies in this visualisation, thus helping them to new standards of health and vitality (see meditation below).

Trust that 'all is well, all manner of things are well and all shall be very well indeed'. Such trust casts out fear and allows love to flow in. Love enables, creates and transforms. Even, and especially, in the face of all your present difficulties, practise love more consistently in your inner and outer lives. Give it out and allow it to flow in. It is the life-force of change.

My love and blessing are with you.

Meditation to Help the Golden Age to Manifest

Make sure that you will be undisturbed. Sit comfortably with your back supported and your body symmetrically arranged. Become aware of the rhythm of your breathing.

Imagine a source of golden light just above your head . . . As you breathe in, draw light into your body from this source . . . Imagine it permeating each bodily area . . . Imagine it flowing through your blood vessels and vitalising your cells . . . Imagine your whole body glowing with golden light ... Open your eyes, if you wish, or simply remember the contents of the room in which you are sitting ... Continue to breathe golden light into your body on each in-breath and on each out-breath breathe it out into the atmosphere ... breathe it into the earth ... breathe it into the furniture ... the walls and ceilings, all the physical substance of your home ... send it out to loved ones and to your pets ... Breathe it into your plants ... include your garden ... the substance of earth itself ... Sense that each particle which begins to glow with this golden light passes its luminosity on to whatever is next to it ... the glow in the earth reaches deeper and deeper ... the glow in each person touches another ... Imagine the whole planet and all its peoples glowing with a warm golden light which carries a vibration of love and causes everything to flourish in peak health and vitality ... When you are ready to do so come back to your everyday surroundings. As you go about your tasks continue to carry a sense of golden light and hope with you ... Let it touch all whom you meet.

The Gildas Prayer

Let Light from the Source shine into the darknesses of earth and bring Healing

Let Love from the Source shine into our hearts and bring Peace and Harmony.

Let the force of Light tempered with Love, enter into our minds that the things of our own creation may be more truly in the image of God.

Let Light and Love, Peace and Strength, Healing and Harmony bring at last that Union with the Source which passes all Understanding.

Let Understanding born of Peace and Harmony, Light and Love, encompass the earth, now and for ever. Amen.

Glossary

Angelic Beings: These are direct reflections of Divine Consciousness. They are intermediaries and guardians helping the Divine plan to manifest on earth. Their hierarchy includes Guardian Angels, Archangels, Cherubim and Seraphim.

The elemental/devic/angelic hierarchy or life-stream may be seen as moving from the Divine consciousness towards earth, while the human stream of consciousness, which includes discarnate guides, may be seen to be moving towards reunification with the Divine. Thus the elemental/devic/angelic hierarchy is separate from humanity. Discarnates are not angels and angels will not take on human form or consciousness. Our Guardian Angels are different from our guides or discarnate mentors.

Anima/Animus: These are Jungian terms (from C. G. Jung the psychologist). An important part of personality integration, whatever our gender, is to come to terms with both the masculine and feminine principles. These are present in each one of us. The inner feminine in a man is called the 'Anima' and the inner masculine in a woman, the 'Animus'.

Archetypes: By dictionary definition these are 'primordial images inherited by all'. Each human society is affected by forces such as peace, war, beauty, justice, wisdom, healing, death, birth, love, power. The essence of these defies definition and we need images, myths, symbols and personifications to help us in understanding the depth and breadth of them. Tarot cards, which have ancient origins, have twenty-two personified or symbolised archetypes in the major arcana. These cover all aspects of human experience.

Ascended Masters: The title comes from esoteric tradition. They are of the human stream of consciousness and have perfected their evolution. Their stems or threads are reunited (see chapter 6). The final step of evolution is reunification with the Source. The Ascended Ones sacrifice that step, in order to maintain enough individuality to be able to help human beings in incarnation and the total evolution of humanity. The original title comes from the patriarchal tradition; 'Ascended Ones' seems more correct since they are beyond gender and sexuality.

Aura: An energy field, which interpenetrates with and radiates out beyond the physical body. It has various frequencies vibrating within it, which are called subtle bodies. Clairvoyantly seen, the aura is full of light, colour and shade. The trained healer or seer sees, within the aura, indications as to the spiritual, mental, physical and emotional state of the individual. Much of the auric colour and energy comes from the chakras.

Between-Life State: The nature of being is eternal. At the end of a lifetime on earth, our essence does not die. Gildas' teachings include belief in reincarnation. The place to which our essence and consciousness goes, before another incarnation is undertaken, is a subtle plane (see also Glossary entry, **Other planes**). Here we are held in a 'between-life state'. We make a review of the life we have most recently lived. Healers, guides and advisers help us to make decisions about future learning from incarnation, but opportunities for learning and service also exist on the other planes.

Chakras: (See diagram, page 94). The word chakrum is Sanskrit and means 'wheel'. Properly speaking chakrum is the singular form and chakra the plural but in the West it is usual to speak of one chakra and many chakras. Much of the colour and energy of the auric field (see also Glossary entry, **aura**), is supplied by the chakras. Clairvoyantly seen they are wheels of light and colour interpenetrating with, affecting and affected by, the physical body. Most chakras carry links to specific parts of the glandular system and might therefore be described as subtle glands.

Most Eastern traditions describe a sevenfold major chakra system, at the same time acknowledging varying large numbers of minor chakras throughout the body. The diagram on page 94 shows the seven major chakras plus the Alter Major, and their positions in relationship to the physical body. They are named in descending order as Crown, Brow, Alter Major, Throat, Heart, Solar Plexus, Sacral and Root. Semantic difficulties can arise simply because there is a variety of terminology, some of which is Eastern and some more Westernised. For instance different teachers use the terms 'Sacral', 'Hara' or 'Spleen' to refer to the chakra which is two fingers below the navel. Confusion of terms around 'Brow', 'Ajna', or 'Third Eye' also occurs.

Chakras from the Solar Plexus upwards are often referred to as 'higher chakras' and the ones below and including the Solar Plexus as 'lower chakras'. These should not be seen as terms of evaluation. They are descriptive of the position of the chakras in relationship to the physical body when upright. There is not a hierarchical system within the chakras, each is part of a team.

There is a central subtle column of energy

interpenetrating with the physical body and running from the crown of the head to the perineum (the area mid-way between the anus and the genitals). Each chakra has petals and a stem. The stems of the Crown and Root chakras are open and are contained within the central column. The other chakras have petals which open into the auric field at the back. The stems usually stay closed but the petals are flexible, opening and closing, vibrating and turning according to the different life situations encountered. A healthy chakra is a flexible chakra. Where there is disease the chakra energies become inflexible or actually blocked. Working with chakras can thus aid physical, mental, emotional and spiritual health.

The original seven chakras carry the colours of the rainbow spectrum. Red for the Root, orange for the Sacral, yellow for the Solar Plexus, green for the Heart, blue for the Throat, indigo for the Brow and violet for the Crown. (The Alter Major is brown). This does not necessarily mean that the chakras *are* these colours, but that they are responsible for that colour note within the chakra team and the auric field. Any colour may be 'seen' or sensed in *any* chakra. It could be said that each chakra has its own full spectrum of colour. The presence, quality and degree of other colours reflects information about ourselves.

Collective Unconscious: This term comes from the work of C. G. Jung, the psychologist. It refers to the collective bank of human experience. Everything which is presently happening in our world affects us, though we are only consciously aware of our own 'little patch'. Moreover, everything which has ever been experienced or accomplished by humanity, historically, is also stored. Myths and symbols can help us to tap into the creative collective unconscious. Nightmares, anxieties and irrational fears may be activated by collective, rather than personal factors.

Colour Healing Temples on Other Planes: (See also Glossary entry **Other Planes**) On the planes where we exist in the 'between-life' state there are healing temples. These are formed of light and colour and have subtle geometric form. Pure translucent colour is used by helpers, guides and angelic beings to enable healing and transformation. Sometimes we may visit these temples in our sleep state, while still in incarnation.

Groups of souls and guides, who are concerned with the expression of form, take part in building, guarding and maintaining these temples. Their structures can be an inspiration to architects on the earth plane. Inspiration is a form of guidance. Buildings of great beauty are harmonious and do not deface the earth landscape. Such buildings are 'inspired creations'. As our aspiration becomes purer, the sacred geometric structures and proportions reflected from these other planes will be used more extensively on the earth plane.

Cosmology (dictionary definition): The science of the universe as a whole. A treatise on the structure and parts of the system of creation.

Devas/Devic beings: These may sometimes be confused with angels. A deva is a good, shining spirit and often very tall. Their concern is with trees, rocks, plants, animals, and the four elements. They are guardians who work to maintain balance in these realms and in the interaction of humanity with the natural kingdoms. They are part of the angelic hierarchy/stream of consciousness. (See also Glossary entry, **Angelic Beings**).

Dimensions: We presently live in a mainly three-dimensional world. Objects have length, breadth and thickness. Pictures and the written word are two-dimensional – though perspective can give art works depth and a three-dimensional impression. The fourth dimension takes in space and light (as in Einstein's relativity theories). The fifth dimension is a 'new' concept, which seems connected with expansion of thought and mind, and freedom from the limitations of time. Travel on thought waves or by de-materialisation and re-materialisation of physical substance becomes possible in the fifth dimension. Once we 'embrace' this dimension, by expansion of our finite minds, the substance of matter will change or be refined.

Discarnates: Technically this term applies to any being or intelligence which is not in a physical body and incarnate on planet earth. In this book it is used to refer to guides and helpers from other planes, who are part of the human stream of consciousness but at present not in incarnation and who have reached a point where their evolution is continuing without the need to reincarnate.

Earth as a Planet of Choice: Creation myths, such as the story of Adam and Eve often include a 'fall' from Divine Grace. The biblical myth in particular sows the seeds which can make us see ourselves as eternally unworthy sinners. Gildas and other guides see the events which led us to take the 'path of knowledge' as a choice which we had the right to make. It is a commitment to evolution and empowerment, to the path which leads eventually to 'wise innocence' rather than protected and naïve innocence.

Evolution then, consists of the necessity to make a series of progressive conscious and responsible choices.

Gildas sees humanity as now approaching a point at which there will be a collective decision to eradicate certain behaviours and possibilities from our range of experience. Thus violence, crime and war would not just be repressed but would no longer exist. When life force is withdrawn, existence ceases.

The other planets and planes do not have the same range of choices available. Maliciously destructive forces do not exist on other planets, therefore the basic choice of good or evil does not apply. Other planetary beings cannot choose to destroy their planets. In one sense they are more in tune with universal harmony; in another sense they have less force, since the power of choice is considerable. Choice also leads to certain confusions, uncertainties and insecurities. Part of our task in enabling positive change lies in taking 'clarity' as a key-word.

Entities: The dictionary definition of the word 'entity' is 'being, existence: something with objective reality'. In spiritual terms the word can be almost interchangeable with 'discarnate'. An entity in this vocabulary is a being without a physical body. It does not necessarily have a negative meaning, though the term has come to be associated with ghosts, hauntings, obsessions and possessions.

Esoteric teaching also states that thoughts have energy. When a thought is strong, or universal enough, it takes on form. It becomes an entity. Thought forms can obviously be positive or negative. To change them, life-force energy must be withdrawn from them. When we get drawn into negative thought patterns we fuel negative thought forms/entities. If we think positively we strengthen positive thought forms/entities.

Extra-Terrestrials: Since the film *ET* this term perhaps needs little explanation! ET's are beings from other planets. They are the same as 'aliens', 'other planetary intelligences' and 'space people'.

Free Will: (See also Glossary entry **Earth as a planet of choice**). There have been many philosophical dissertations on the nature of free will. The question is: Do we really have free choice of action or are all our lives and events preordained, predetermined or predestined?

Gildas takes the view that our higher selves (see chapter 6), have free will, and that only a certain proportion of the future can be accurately 'seen' or forecast. The personality has free will within the circumspection of governing choices which the higher self has already made. The personality achieves spiritual harmony when it willingly and gracefully surrenders to the higher will and purpose.

Free Writing: This is writing which is just allowed to flow freely without criticism. Judgement is suspended until the piece is read through. It is not the same as automatic writing which is done in a trance state with the pen seeming to move itself.

Gaia: A mythical name for planet earth. Current 'Gaia theory' imbues the planet with a consciousness of its own. If human beings continue to abuse Gaia and her resources, then she will break the bond between herself and humanity. *Her* survival mechanism will cause her to become hostile to the parasitic force which is threatening to destroy her. Conditions on earth will become unsuitable for human habitation. Gaia will not sacrifice herself for humanity.

Gildas sometimes speaks of earth as 'Gaia' and emphasises the need for respect for this living being, but he sees some things, such as global warming as the beginning of 'mutational change'. He reminds us to be mindful of our actions and warns against complacency but maintains a positive view of our future on earth.

Interface: This is a term most often used to describe the area in which two different belief systems meet and overlap. Gildas speaks of an 'interface' between planes. There is not a rigid boundary between one plane and the next. Thus we can stay safely grounded in our own reality and also meet our guides in area of interface between their planes and ours. Both have to make a journey, but there is a safe meeting area.

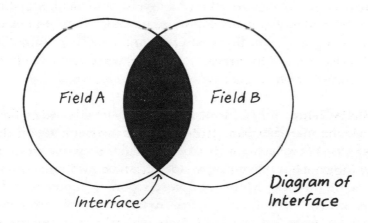

Diagram of Interface

Karma: The original law of cause and effect (which defies 'nutshell' definition). 'As you sow, so shall you reap', gives a basic but over-simplified idea of it. Belief in karma goes alongside belief in reincarnation and personal, progressive evolution. The tendency is to see karma as being something troublesome or heavy which needs to be overcome during a specific lifetime – but giftedness or innate wisdom are positive karmic attributes.

Myth: Confusion may arise over the use of this word, since one of its meanings is 'a figment: a commonly held belief which is untrue or without foundation'. The other meaning and the sense in which it is used in this book is 'an ancient traditional story of gods or heroes, offering explanation of some fact or phenomenon: a story with hidden meaning'.

Myths can be heard or revealed in different ways at one and the same time. Those who want entertainment hear a delightful story. Those who seek deeper meaning are moved by the symbolism to an understanding which goes beyond the intellect. The interface (see entry above), between science and myth is relatively unformed, whereas that between religion and myth is hazy and confused. Myth is not dogmatic but fluid and imaginative. It contains the richness of collective and racial experience and enables a passage between conscious and unconscious realities.

Other Planes: When incarnate, our existence is dependent upon the material plane, where things have substance and solidity. Yet we are complex beings and if we pause to study the range of our perceptions, not all can be explained by the laws of physics. Many people encounter 'other-worldly phenomena' from near-death experiences to prophetic dreams, from sensing 'atmospheres' in old buildings to telepathic communication with a loved one, either alive or dead.

Esoteric teaching tells us that there are at least six other planes of experience, which are not just phenomena of perception but actual territories. The nearest to us is the etheric plane, which in itself is largely an interface between the material and the astral plane. This latter is divided into a number of layers or regions. The lower astral is largely populated with negative thought forms. (It is probably the region which severe alcoholics experience when they have DTs or drug users when they have a 'bad trip'.) The higher levels of the astral plane are where we meet our guides and where there are temples of light and healing and beautiful subtle landscapes. We may visit the astral planes in our dreams, each night, as well as being able to travel there in the altered state of consciousness induced by meditation. Beyond the astral plane are the feeling plane, the lower and higher mental planes and the causal plane. (Names for each of the planes may vary from teacher to teacher, those used here are as given by Gildas.)

Psyche: Analytic and transpersonal psychologies have shown how complex the human personality is. The psyche refers to the total being, with all its drives, needs, conflicts, disease, health, gifts and potential.

Reunification with the Twin Stem or Strand: The original spark of individual soul consciousness which comes from the Source splits into two aspects, which remain loosely joined (see chapter 6). When each stem or strand has completed its journey of evolution, the two parts blend together again, and either join the Ascended Ones or are reabsorbed into the Source, thus enriching the Source itself.

Shadow: The part of the 'I' which we do not admit into full consciousness. That which is unconscious, undefined, formless, dark, shadowy and without concept. The unknown. (See also chapter 6.)

Spiritual Family: In the 'organisation' of souls, we are divided into groups and families. When other members of our spiritual or soul family are in incarnation with us we usually 'recognise' them and form deep and inspiring friendships or relationships with them. The genetic family into which we are born does not necessarily contain members of our spiritual family. Children, parents, siblings, may be very different in spiritual nature and origin. We may not find our 'real' family until comparatively late in life.

Sub-personalities: This is a term used by the transpersonal psychologist 'Assagioli' to describe and explain some of the complexities of, and tensions within, our personalities. On separate occasions, different motives, traits, attitudes, purposes and value systems may operate in us and affect the way in which we handle life. We are multifaceted. At times we may fear that we are 'split personalities' or be anxious about the nature of our identities. We all have sub-personalities, distinct universes, within ourselves, each with their own story to tell. Some of them may be seen as 'survival mechanisms'. If we are tied to a job we do not enjoy, the mask we wear, or the style we bring to that situation may be our saving grace.

Discovering and integrating sub-personalities so that they all live happily together within us and are in happy communication with the central 'I', is one of the most important tasks in personal growth.

Symbol: Is that which represents something else. It is usually pictorial or imaginative. C. G. Jung explains that symbols are different from signs. The familiar red cross on a white background signs to us that 'first aid' is at hand. The *symbol* of the red cross holds a greater richness: the cross itself is an ancient symbol for the cardinal points, the seasons, and mind, body, emotions and spirit; the cross on a white background is both the sign of the crusaders and the flag of St George. Seeing the red cross as a symbol rather than a sign opens up many possibilities of meaning.

When we use our inner worlds, or study our dreams, all manner of images and symbols may appear. They are not subject to facile interpretation, because of their richness. C. G. Jung said: 'It is important to *have* a symbol.' If we 'live alongside it' and reflect on what it means to us the symbol will gradually reveal its meaning. When referring to a dictionary of symbols it is important to use one which does not give categoric definitions. Symbols help us in bringing valuable unconscious material into awareness.

Yin and Yang: These are Chinese words for the basic but opposite aspects of creation. Yin is receptive, feminine and dark. Yang is active, masculine and light. In the traditional yin/yang symbol one black and one white fish-like shape nestle together to form a perfect circle. The eye of the black shape is white and of the white shape black, showing that the seed of each is contained in the other.

Bibliography

Books by Ruth White

(The first three titles with Mary Swainson)
Gildas Communicates, C.W. Daniel Co. Ltd
Seven Inner Journeys, C.W. Daniel Co. Ltd
The Healing Spectrum, C.W. Daniel Co. Ltd
A Question of Guidance, C.W. Daniel Co. Ltd
Working With Your Chakras, Piatkus Books

Recommended Reading

Cooper, C.J., *The Aquarian Dictionary of Festivals*, Aquarian
Cooper, C.J., *An Illustrated Encyclopaedia of Symbols,*
  Thames and Hudson
C.G. Jung, *Man and his Symbols,* Aldus Books
Ferrucci, Pierro (Disciple of Assagioli), *What We May Be,*
  Thorsons Publishing Group
Bailey, Alice, *Discipleship in the New Age*, The Lucius
  Trust

Index